Overtaken

By
R.W.K. Clark

Published in the United States by Clarkltd.
Po Box 45313 Rio Rancho, NM 87174
info@clarkltd.com

Edition 1

United States Copyright Office
TX8-278-943 May 2016

Library of Congress Control Number
LCCN: 2017907098

International Standard Book Numbers
ISBN-13: 978-1948312004 (Paperback)
ISBN-13: 978-0692489314 (Paperback)
ISBN-13: 978-1948312127 (Hardback)
ASIN: B011Z9UBLM (Kindle)

/200801

CONTENTS

ACKNOWLEDGMENTS

I dedicate this novel to my wonderful readers and for all the amazing people I've met and those I haven't. To my family and loved ones, all your support will not be forgotten.

This book was made possible by reviews from readers like you.

Thank you

R.W.K. Clark

PROLOGUE

Huck Brown looked up at the sky as he pumped gasoline into the sedan that sat at the pump before him. Not too many service stations pumped your gas anymore, and Huck was proud to work for one that still took customer service seriously. You don't make commuters in business suits do things like handle gas pumps. Who wants to go to work smelling like petrol, anyway?

The sky was a beautiful shade of blue, with tinges of violet as it neared the earth. Perfect! This was going to be a day like no other, a day to remember. Already it reminded him of those early mornings when he and his brother Cayden would walk to school just as the sun was lighting the sky. In all his twenty-nine years, this was likely one of his favorites and most often recalled, memories. The butterflies, the dew on the grass, and the anticipation of seeing Violet Hanson were all overwhelming to his mind.

The pump clicked off in his hands, and he turned, still deep in thought, to replace it into the pump unit itself. He flipped the lock and looked at the sky again. It seemed like it was getting a bit darker to the north. He didn't recall any less-than-desirable forecasts on the news or radio. Must just be a few sparse clouds.

He walked to the front of the sedan and tapped on the driver's side window. "Did you want me to check the oil for you today?" The woman inside smiled pleasantly and shook her head. She was dressed in a purple jumper with a silky white shirt underneath, and she wore eyeglasses that had to be worth a small fortune.

Whatever suits your hoity-toity ass then, thought Huck. He never had been a fan for those who acted like you were their servant. He smiled back with great heartfelt love and proceeded to take the windshield washer blade out of the bucket next to the pumps so he could wash her windshield. A loud, brief honk brought him to reality, and he looked at the woman inside the car. She was shaking her head while simultaneously waving him aside impatiently.

"Well, screw you very much lady," he said, nodding while he tipped his dirty black NASCAR hat in her direction. "I have cigarettes with my name on them waiting to be smoked, you old hag."

Huck watched with a bit of distaste as the car drove hastily out of the lot; thank goodness for prepay. These people think the whole world is about them; screw the rest of us. He looked up to the sky again. The gray was now taking on a hue that was much closer to black in color, and it was sharp in contrast against the blue sky which surrounded it. It even seemed to be moving rapidly in his direction. Out loud he asked himself,

"What the heck kinda storm is this gonna be?"

He turned to walk back into the station, subconsciously humming along to the Bee Gees tune playing over the speakers which were set into the overhang which housed the pumps. "You should be dan-cin', yeah!" His feet got a bit out of control as he ripped off a couple of John Travolta steps. He would have been good if he had really tried.

He walked first around to the restroom which was located at the side of the building. He fished in his pocket for his keys and opened the door. Reaching inside, he flipped the light on and entered the area, smelling and looking around at the same time. Empty.

He stopped at the mirror and took a look, removing his NASCAR hat and running his fingers through his greasy mop of light brown, unkempt hair. "Ya know, Huck, if your mama would have named you anything else, you would have had a serious chance at the limelight!" His light blue eyes shone as he smiled broadly, revealing four missing teeth along his bottom row. His smile straightened up immediately. "At least, if you had seen a dentist too." He smiled again, this time at his own humor.

Huck walked over to the urinal conveniently located in the co-ed bathroom just for studs like himself, and he did his business in little to no time. He didn't really bother to wash his hands, but for the sake of conscience, he rinsed them off pretty good. Mama would have been proud. Not too many of his Harrisville, Illinois friends would have had the courtesy to do the same and then touch a gas pump. This was because Huck had real class.

He dried his hands on the last brown paper towel in the dispenser, making a mental note to send Dickie, the gofer here at the pump-n-jump, out with a new stack of towels as soon as he got back in. He tossed the wadded up paper waste into the trash bin and thought, "Have him take the trash out of here too." With that, he turned the knob on the restroom door and went back out into the April day.

But the sun was no longer shining, and the sky was no bluer than a room with no lightbulbs or candles. It was just damn dark.

Huck snapped his neck back almost immediately to observe what he thought was a storm-filled sky. Instead, he observed a slate-gray object which nearly filled the entire area above. Here and there the twinkle of what appeared to be stars was dispersed over the surface of the gray.

"What the heck…"

Huck took a sharp breath in as his eyes began to make out what he was really seeing. The entire sky over Harrisville, Illinois was filled with what looked to this uneducated hick to be a… massive spaceship.

∞

June Ellison stood from her desk at the TransCoverage Insurance Headquarters in Mesa, Arizona. She enjoyed a long leisurely stretch. It may be only 2:00pm here, but she felt like she had been working for the last three days straight. It certainly didn't help that she had twin girls at home, and they were under a year old at that. She was simply flipping exhausted all the time!

She walked away from her desk and headed for the breakroom. She hated her job, filing data on claim investigations. It was the same; day after day, month after month, and year after year. Nothing changed: they were either legitimate claims, or they were attempting to rip TransCoverage off for chunks of dough. Frankly, she thought it would be worth it if they could get away with it. Some of the premiums these people paid on their policies were enough to incite larceny if she had ever seen it, and TransCoverage seemed to rarely be the one making the payoff. At least, that was how it appeared to her.

She stirred liquid creamer into her hot java, thinking that if caffeine and sugar together could not get her to move her ass, nothing could. For good measure, she plopped another dollop of the creamer in and continued to vigorously stir. It certainly couldn't hurt. She still had three more hours to go before her shackles were unlocked. Her freedom was nonetheless imminent.

June took her steep cup of joe and headed to the outdoor employee break area. She didn't smoke, but from the windows, the day looked ravishing. It was warm and sunny, even better than she would have hoped for a brand new spring day in April. She simply had to have a taste. She had listened to the radio on the way to work, and the weather forecast was adamant: it would reach sixty degrees! She was bound and determined to have even the tiniest taste. As she stepped outside, she was initially oblivious to her co-workers gathered at the handrail which served to keep people safe from falling six inches to the hard concrete below. She smiled to herself at the crowd they formed, then realized that there was, indeed, a crowd there, and for no apparent reason.

Observing the crowd briefly, June realized they were all looking at the sky, and in the same moment she realized how dismally dark it was for this time of day. Was it going to storm? Reality did not want to kick in and support her vision, so she continued to struggle to make mental sense of the strange behavior she was seeing. "What's going on, everybody?" She asked as she made her way over to the group of people she lightly referred to as friends.

As her eyes went up to see what they were so intently staring at, she sucked in her breath. "What in the name of….?" The coffee fell from her hand without her realization. She could make no more sense of what was in the sky than she could of the dark afternoon.

A dark gray, or almost black, crescent filled the entire skyline, except for a small sliver of blue which sat to the north. From the look of things, this sliver was closing fast. The gray was covered with twinkling lights. "Look at the stars…" was all she managed to get out before the entire group began to descend into chaos.

Before the screams of disorganization began, she was able to get a good hard look at the sky, or at least, what appeared to be the sky at first sight. This was no sky at all; if it was, it was made of metal. She sucked in another deep breath just as the sliver of blue disappeared from her vision for good.

All June Ellison could do was scream loudly, and for as long, as she possibly could.

R.W.K. Clark

CHAPTER 1

Joshua Nichols sat at the desk in his office staring blankly at his computer screen. He held a pen in his right hand and tapped it rhythmically against his thigh to the beat of a pop song playing out of his mp3 dock. He was looking at virtually nothing. At least, nothing he was seeing was registering. So much for his mid-day burst of energy. What a day to cut back on coffee.

Josh had been working for the United States government for three years as a software engineer, writing code and cleaning up their systems. Most of his co-workers resented him a bit; he was only 23, very young for such a position. He had been considered a prodigy, graduating college at 20 with honors. The government had been on top of their game, recruiting him, grooming him, and wiping the wetness from behind his ears as they held his hand. He learned to walk on his own and learned to keep his distance from the old fogies. Regardless of the nastiness, he had made a name for himself here, and while they didn't have to like him, they did show him respect.

He heard chaos going on behind him and turned from his computer. People were rushing around, and a few of the women had a confused, panicky look on their faces. He had his door closed; he could make out no real words, but the scene through the blinds said it all. Something was definitely out of the ordinary. ISIS? Other terrorist attacks? He should have gone to med school like his dear mother wanted him to.

Josh stood from his seat at his desk and, opening his office door, entered the ado which grew increasingly stronger. Some were speed walking from point 'A' to point 'B'; others were jabbering to whoever was next to them. All had panic-stricken looks upon their faces.

He touched the arm of Jill Wilson, a thirty-something-year-old who worked at the main desk on their floor screening visitors. "Jill, what the heck is going on here?" She looked at him as though he had lost his mind.

"What do you mean? Look out the window, Josh! I have to take these messages to Holbrook so they can be forwarded to the governor. We are being invaded!" Just like that, she took off full speed ahead toward the elevator at the end of the hall. Josh shook his head as if trying to clear it, then walked to the end of the hall himself to look out the window.

His first thought as he approached the window was, when did they tint these windows? It was much darker than he remembered it, but he rarely paid the windows any mind. He walked up to the window and looked out.

People ran all over the street like they had lost their minds. The sky was completely dark and filled with stars. There was no sun, and there were no clouds; the sky was as slate. The commotion on the street, from what Josh could tell by just looking, was out of control, and he could not wrap his mind around what was going on at all.

"It's a spaceship! Josh, it's a spaceship!" The voice behind him was that of Drew, a mid-level supervisor on his floor.

"What do you mean, it's a spaceship?" This guy was obviously nipping the bottle when he was behind closed doors. "The sky is overcast, looks like a big storm…"

Drew's eyes were completely panic-stricken. "Didn't you listen to the news? Don't you have a radio at your desk?" His voice had gone from one tinted with desperation to a high nasal whine, and his words fell out of his mouth at an increasing pace. "This isn't the only one. This isn't a storm!" He turned on his heel and headed for the fire stairs; he wasn't even going to consider the elevator.

Josh shook his head, more to clear the cobwebs of confusion than to express disgust at Drew's adolescent behavior. What the heck was going on? As though he were in a trance, he made his way back to his office to pull up the radio on his computer and see what he could learn. He didn't even make it to his office before noticing a small group of co-workers in the smaller office next door, gathered around the desk inside listening to a radio.

"…State and federal authorities claim. Again, it appears that a massive flying vessel has emerged, not only over the Washington, DC area, but reports have been received stating similar vessels are hovering over Baltimore, Chicago, Dallas-Fort Worth, Seattle, Phoenix, and Sacramento. According to distant news sources, Paris, Luxembourg, and London are also under the shadow of unknown ships. Stay tuned for updates from our news source." The thread then went to a repetitive alert sound, followed by an announcement for a presidential address in two minutes. Josh slid down the wall of the office next to the door and made himself as comfortable as possible. He wanted more details.

He had become oblivious to the ranting and screaming, as well as all of the running around going on right outside the door, just as the others listening to the newscast were. Even though a commercial was emitting from the small, antique-looking transistor type radio, all of them continued to stare at it, waiting for the next broadcast with fear and disbelief in their eyes.

It seemed like a lifetime before the announcer came on and introduced an emergency state of the union address by President Andrew Mason. He began to speak clearly and calmly, addressing the current alleged spaceship situation.

"As of this afternoon, we have come to experience what many are referring to as an alien invasion. Now, while it appears that we are indeed being visited, there has currently been no communication attempts on the part of our guests, and we are having no trouble with broadcasting efforts here in the states. The important thing is to not panic. We recommend you remain in your homes if possible. If you are at work, stay at work.

We are confident that we will be able to clear up the confusion surrounding the current situation, and as soon as that takes place, we will relate all information to you as well. In the meantime, stay inside and keep your televisions and radios tuned into your preferred channels for updates. Thank you." He was finished speaking as quickly as he had begun, and the announcer took over once again.

"That was President Mason asking citizens to stay where they are or get to a safe place indoors as soon as possible. Keep your radios and TVs tuned in for frequent updates on the situation. It appears as if the 'life on other planets' question has been answered for us. This is Bob Riley for WDCX news." Josh had begun to phase out his words right away and rose to get to his office to contact his family and find out their situation.

Josh was from a small town in Iowa, which boasted around 8,000 residents. He had always loved technology. His graduating early, at the top of his high school class, had made a full ride scholarship possible. He took his computer studies very seriously and was drafted by the government while he was still in the middle of his final year at the University of Iowa in Iowa City. His parents would never have been able to afford the furthering of his education, much less visit him had he not stayed so close while in college. His mother had been completely shattered when she learned he would live and work in DC. His father had been so proud his chest swelled. After all, the man had worked by the sweat of his brow his entire life, days at the railroad and nights at a nearby factory which made medical equipment.

Mom had stayed home, thus explaining the separation anxiety she experienced when Josh left Iowa. The first thought in his mind was to let them know he was okay, then to find out what they were enduring. Could they see a ship from where they were? How big were these things, really? It appeared to him from the window that they completely filled the sky above. Was it one or many? There were simply too many questions to satisfy with the scant information he had gathered so far.

He picked up his office phone and called his parents' house phone. It rang six times before the voicemail feature answered, his father's voice telling him how sorry he was to miss his call, and if he left a message, his father or mother would gladly get back to him as soon as possible. Josh didn't bother. Instead, he pushed the button on the cradle and hung up, released it, and dialed the number again. His father answered on the second ring.

"Hello?" His voice was not the solid, steady one Josh was accustomed to, the voice of reason. Instead, it was the voice of a very frightened man trying to hold it together.

"Dad, it's Josh." His parents did not use caller ID. They didn't have anyone to avoid. "I wanted to let you know I'm okay. What is happening there?"

Robert Nichols released a ragged breath. "Josh, thank goodness. Mom, it's Josh." His dad and mom always referred to each other just that way. He couldn't recall them ever calling each other by their first names.

He could hear his mother in the background. "Let me talk to him, Bob." There was noise as his dad handed the phone over, and then his mother was sobbing into the phone.

"Josh, where are you? Are you okay? They said a ship is directly over Washington. Can you see it? Are you safe? Have you been hurt? I would say the best thing is for you to come home now. Don't even risk being there another moment. Joshua? Are you listening, Josh?" Even in the midst of all the anxiety, her words brought a smile to his face. She was as panicked as they come.

"Mother, I can't just leave. I am at work, I am safe. With this going on, I imagine they will need me here. You need to breathe in and out. Tell me what is happening there." He had to make himself be still to give her an opportunity to answer.

She drew a deep breath and let it out. He heard her do it again. "We can see a ship south of here, far away though. Josh, it's massive! Overwhelming! I can't even bear to look out the window. Your father wants to speak to you. I love you, and I want you to come home!"

"Mom, as soon as we all know more about what is going on, and I know it is safe, I will come. Let me talk to dad." More shuffling, then his dad was back on the line.

"So you have one right over you? We have clear sky

here, but the horizon to the south is full of one. You can't see past it, but it's pretty far from us. It just seems to be sitting there. What have you heard, Josh?" Josh thought about his answer. From the way it sounded, he didn't know any more than they.

He took a breath. "Well, I know there are several, and it sounds like they are positioned with intent. It would be interesting to know what is really going on. I have a hard time believing that the powers that be have heard nothing. But I don't want to hang on the line for long, Dad. I want to get the radio on and listen for updates. You have yours on, right? Or the TV, or something?"

"Yes. Your mother won't watch, and I don't want her to. But I need to. Keep in constant touch, please Josh. Don't make us worry now."

Josh nodded absentmindedly. "The same goes for you. I'll talk to you soon, and I love you both."

After giving his dad time to say goodbye, he hung up the phone and got his cell out. He tuned in using the digital radio app he had on it and popped it into the dock so he could hear more clearly. He closed his office door, sat at his desk, and waited for the word.

CHAPTER 2

"Kamryn, wake up! Someone is knocking at the door!" Melissa's words jolted her awake, and she sat straight up, swinging her legs to the floor, completely alert.

She shook the cobwebs out of her head. "Did you ask who it was?"

"I didn't say anything, what, after the last time?" Melissa's face looked petrified and grief-stricken. The last time she was referred to; she opened the door to the police, and Kamryn was arrested for her extra-curricular computer hacking activities.

They were harmless enough, at least in her opinion. She mostly hacked away for personal entertainment. It wasn't her fault that the government, colleges, and other people didn't like it. She was bored; besides that, she was good at it.

They knocked again, this time Kamryn was able to hear it clearly. This was not your regulation five rap cop knock. This was done with persistence which bordered on desperation. Who the heck could it be? She glanced at the clock. It was 11:47 at night. Who could be at the door other than the cops? But she hadn't done any overt, traceable hacking all day.

She rose from her bed and slowly tip-toed over to the door. Melissa sat on the foot of her bed, her eyes glued to Kamryn as she made her way. Her eyes would shift from Kamryn to the door and back every couple of seconds.

When Kamryn got to the door, she lowered herself to the lighted crack beneath. One set of feet on the other side. Slowly she stood and glanced at Melissa. She didn't have a tendency to think too clearly in situations such as these. She had made an unwarranted trip to jail with Kamryn the last time, due to guilt by association, Kamryn felt the need to be gentle with her.

"It's only one person. I think we're good." She then raised her voice a bit, making sure she sounded wide awake. "Who is it?"

There was a pause. "Kamryn, it's Chuck. You need to let me in!" She immediately began to fiddle with the deadbolt and chain to let him in. Chuck was her main road dog when it came to her source of fun and games.

As she opened the door, Chuck pretty much fell into the one-room apartment. His shaggy brown hair was wet with sweat, and his complexion was flushed. He was breathing hard.

"Chuck, what are you doing? Is there trouble? What's going on? It's after eleven, dude!" He looked around the room erratically, his breathing uneven and raspy.

"Kamryn, there are ships! They are hovering all around, all over the planet! Are you listening? We need to get out of here!" Now she found herself amused with him, and thought he likely had tried some new drug one of his grungy friends was always bringing around.

"Chuck, if they are all over the world, where do you think you should run to?" A smile tugged at the corners of her mouth, but she saw that he was genuinely upset. She didn't want to agitate him any further, but her question was doing just that. It was best to rein him in now. "Okay, okay, Chuck. Show me."

With that, he grabbed her by the hand and led her past Melissa, who sat with a wide-eyed look on her bed, to the window. He grabbed the string and raised the vertical blind almost violently. All she could see was darkness above. She looked back toward Chuck. "It's the night sky, friend."

He began to violently shake his head. "That's because it's nighttime! Look on the street. People are going crazy. This isn't just me, Kam." He let out a frustrated growl and jerked her by the arm to the door of the room.

"Hey! Careful! You're hurting me!" He didn't seem to hear her, or else he didn't care. She kept up with him as he led her down the stairs to the lobby of the building, her bare feet slapping the cold tile as they went. "Look, Chuck, why don't you try to get some sleep. You'll feel better in the morning."

He continued to walk, and without looking at her, said in the calmest voice he had used since he arrived, "I don't know if I'll ever sleep again, dude."

His very tone sent a chill up her spine, though she

didn't know why. He put his hand out and pushed on the entrance to the building. It swung outward, and he pulled her into the cool night air.

"Now, look up."

Kamryn did so immediately, simply in response, but she was not prepared for what she saw. Sure, she had been sleeping quite a bit lately. She had been a bit depressed since the arrest, but how had she missed something like this?

The sky was mostly dark, except for the array of tiny, twinkling lights which were scattered over its surface with no rhyme or reason. There were spotlights, though, shining from the Baltimore ground into the sky, and what they illuminated made no sense to her mind. A slate-gray surface seemed to fill what she had thought was the sky. It was vast, and as the spotlights moved over its surface, it appeared there was no end in sight.

He stared at her face as she looked upward, but she was oblivious to his observation. All she knew was what she saw, and she was subconsciously aware that her mouth was hanging wide open, but she just didn't have enough control over herself to close it. She nearly pissed down her leg, and her bowels felt loose and watery.

Now Chuck looked up at the massive thing with her. "It's been all over the radio and TV. This is not the only one, there are several, all around the world." He pulled his eyes back to her. "What have you been doing all day? Sleeping?"

Kamryn held her eyes on the gargantuan thing above, but her mind went back to getting out of jail at four in the morning. She was scared, depressed, and facing some fairly serious charges. She had been told the Feds were considering charging her with espionage. All she wanted to do was sleep, and when she got home, she had immediately escaped to the land of her dreams. Melissa had fallen out too; she had seen her when she got up to relieve herself at around five-thirty in the afternoon. Besides, they didn't have television, and the radio was never on while they slept. How was she to know?

Finally, she dragged her eyes from the ship and looked over at Chuck. "How many? Ships? How many are there?"

He shook his head and looked back up. He was very calm now, almost hypnotized. "I'm not sure, but I know of four or five in the States' skyspace. They are saying they are all around the world."

"Come back upstairs," She tugged his arm in the direction of the building, pulling him back to reality along with it. They both went back through the main door and up the stairs to her abode.

When they entered, they found Melissa asleep again, balled up under a blanket on the couch. "Shhh. Let's not wake her up. She has never been the picture of emotional stability. Over here." They went into the far corner, away from sleeping Melissa, where Kamryn plopped down in a single armchair. Chuck rested his butt on the floor before her.

She turned a knob on a small boom box that threatened to be as old as she, which was a ripe twenty-five years of age. She didn't have to worry about finding the news on the radio because it was on every channel on the dial. She met Chuck's gaze as they listened to the tinny voice which emitted from the unit. It was just past midnight.

"As of yet, no word has been given either federally or on the state home front regarding the visitors, as they are being called. Government authorities, including President Mason, have clearly stated that any communication attempts on the part of those inside the ships will be reported. They have been overhead for over seven hours, with no reports from any of the areas witnessing this groundbreaking event…"

Kamryn spun the knob, tuning the dial to another channel. "This is Fran Crosby with WXRI, Rock 102. We are still awaiting word regarding the visitors. London states they have experienced a bit of disruption to their airwaves, but all other locations report nothing similar in any way. Right now it is recommended that we continue to stay safely indoors and wait for word from either local, state, or federal authorities. This is Fran Crosby, stay tuned to WXRI, Rock 102 for information."

Kamryn turned the radio off. "It's real?" That was all she could muster, but her thoughts were much clearer. Maybe she wouldn't have to deal with all these hacking charges after all. She knew it was a selfish way of thinking, but she was a selfish person, and she would be the first to admit it.

"Kamryn, I don't think the entire world is trying to prank us. Everyone is scared to death. Look, I have to get home and check on my mom and sister. I'm calmer now, but I think you should stay inside with the radio on, and maybe you should think about how you are going to talk to scatterbrained Melissa about all of this." Chuck held her eyes while he talked, making sure his words were registering.

She nodded, muttering a powerless, "Thanks, Chuck" as he walked out the door. He locked it behind him and made sure it was securely shut.

Kamryn considered her life and the circumstances around her. Her own parents had been killed during a mountain climbing excursion when she was very young, and she had been taken in by an aunt and uncle on her mother's side until she was 13. They had abused her in every way imaginable, and the only comfort she had in this world was technology. She was equipped to find out anyone's social security number, history, or any other information she wanted. She was not really armed to deal with this, and she had no idea how.

She walked into the bathroom and pulled her hair up into a ponytail. This was her preparation to go online.

After checking on Melissa, she booted up her system and tapped into the Wi-Fi belonging to the guy down the hall. Thankfully, she grinned, it was unlimited, or she would have been busted for this long ago. She would need all the time she could get.

She was going to hack into Washington's computer system. She was going to find out what was going on because after all, the entire world knew they were liars on the grandest scale.

CHAPTER 3

Dawn brought many changes to the world.

Those who had actually listened to the directions to stay inside, remained there, sleep robbed from their eyes and minds. Those who had chosen to defy government orders managed to loot, pillage, and plunder all through the night, and they had no fear of apprehension; the police were basically scared to death to come out. Only those in drug or alcohol induced hazes, or had the hearts of true criminals, braved the uncertainty which hovered above.

Josh Nichols had remained at his office all night, listening to the news, comforting hysterical people, and attempting to use what little pull he had to get information, but to no avail. He managed to get a bit of work done and tried to put all of the focus he could into his work, but writing code was simply not distracting enough when it came to a worldwide alien invasion, even of the most seemingly benevolent sort. As of the rising of the sun, none of the circumstances had changed whatsoever.

Kamryn Reynolds had used the remainder of her night breaking into the government's highly secure system from the comfort of her shabby one-room apartment, listening to her friend Melissa snore lightly without a care in the world. While the actual hacking had taken up much of the night, she did manage to wrap her eyes around some pertinent information that was petrifying. This was around 5:30 in the morning, just as the sun was making love to the horizon, or at least, what little could be seen of it by any of Earth's inhabitants.

The government had indeed been lying. There had been communication, but most of the records kept thus far were encrypted so well that it would take Kam hours to bust the code. What she did get out of the data she had found is that the visitors had not only made contact, they had made demands.

It appeared, as far as she could tell, that these beings were nothing less than scavengers. They desired our resources, particularly the abundance of precious metals which were found here, but their goals were not limited to this. The main point was that every plan they had, every scheme, was solely dependent on the entirety of the human population being gone from the face of the earth. From what she could tell, they were not interested in total genocide. They wanted to kill off only the weak, the helpless, the worthless.

That was really all she could deduce, but the deductions she made had her blood running cold and her skin covered in gooseflesh. One question ran through her mind again and again: could this be real? The answer was a resounding "yes."

Melissa woke at around six that morning to use the bathroom, and Kam had barely heard her, even in the single room. She was completely distracted with thoughts of what she could do to save her own life, what steps she should and would take to survive this horrid experience.

"Have you been up all night?" Melissa stood behind her, one hand on the wall for balance, her long, mousy brown hair mussed all around her face.

Kamryn turned to her with a sharp jerk. Once Melissa's presence registered, she smiled at her comfortingly. "Yeah. I guess after Chuck left, I couldn't get back to sleep. How was your rest?"

Melissa turned and headed to the small bathroom. "Good. I think I might be done. What the heck was his problem, anyway? I thought maybe he had been smoking something."

"No, he was clear," said Kam as she thought her words through. "He wanted to let me know about some 'co-workers' that got busted the same night as me. He thought they might have had loose lips, and he just wanted to talk alone." How easily the lie had sprung from her lips. Maybe she should have been an actress.

The toilet flushed, and Melissa appeared once again, pulling a pair of faded and torn skinny jeans over her nearly emaciated frame. "Who was it?"

"No one you know," replied Kam. "Just some old-schoolers I have known since I was younger." Another lie. She may have been a hacker, but lying to close friends was not something she had ever practiced, and she felt a pang of guilt. "So, what are your plans for the day? Anything?"

"Actually, I thought I would head up to the Jiffy Mart for an egg and sausage English muffin. Do you want something?"

A rush of panic coursed through Kam's already stressed body. She couldn't put it off. They would need to talk.

"No, Mel. Listen, sit down here for a minute, would you?" Melissa gave her an unsure look; maybe it was the sound of Kam's voice that put the doubt in her eyes. She didn't argue, rather, she sat down on the edge of Kam's bed, about three feet away from where Kam sat in the chair with her laptop now next to her feet on the floor.

"What's up? You don't have any money? I have enough to cover you if you're hungry." Something must have been telling Melissa that this was not the problem, because her eyes remained wide and apprehensive.

Kamryn shook her head and looked down at the floor. "No, I'm not hungry. Look, I lied to you a minute ago. Chuck didn't come last night to tell me someone had snitched me out." She watched her friend's face carefully. "He came with much more serious news."

"What's up? Are we in bigger trouble than we thought?"

Kam nodded. "Yes, but not the kind of trouble you

think." She paused, trying to sort out her thoughts and put her words together appropriately for the listener. "Melissa, alien ships have come to Earth."

Melissa's face screwed up into a smile. "You're goofy!" With that, she began to belly laugh. "What the heck, Kam. What kind of mood did you get out of bed in? That's hilarious!"

Kamryn sat, unsmiling, in her chair. She let Mel have her good morning laugh, but while the girl was still winding down her chuckles, Kam rose, took her by the hand, and said, "Come here a minute."

She led her to the window. The day, while not bright, was lit much better than the scene the night before. She stepped back so Melissa could get a look.

Mel stood agape at the open window. Tears formed, she began to shake, and she screamed a blood-curdling scream.

∞

Josh was sitting at his desk listening to the radio when Gary Jimmerson appeared at the door behind him, tapping gently. He spun in his chair, the soft sound startling him.

"What's up, Gary?" Gary was one of the supervisors on his floor.

He smiled grimly at Josh. "Pretty early. No one wants to see their boss at seven in the morning, and you were hard at work, so it seems." Josh nodded in response, not taking his eyes off Gary for a second. "I didn't come to see if you were working. I came to tell you that the president wants all federal employees gathered in their respective buildings in conference rooms. He is going to address us via closed-circuit regarding the visitors."

Josh responded with a simple, "I'll be right there." He turned off his monitor as Gary nodded curtly and left his office. It took him a moment to pull himself together by running a comb through his hair and pausing to clear his mind. It seemed futile to pull himself together mentally. After all, who knew what would happen in the next few moments, much less tomorrow. Alien ships were surrounding the entire world. Nothing seemed quite as unsure to him as the future did right now.

Finally, Josh shook himself out of his confused and apprehensive daze and stood from his desk. He didn't want to miss the interoffice address. He needed to know as much about what was going on as he could learn and so far, this was the only way he could begin to do that.

The conference room for his division's building was located one floor down, and like so many of his co-workers, Josh did not feel comfortable taking the elevator. Countless people were taking the stairs, and he was afraid he would miss the address, so he tried his best to make his way down by side-stepping the shufflers. He arrived at the massive conference room to find it filled to capacity and flowing over. The large viewing screen was in the front of the room, and while there was excessive murmuring going on between the workers, nearly all eyes were glued to it, waiting for

Andrew Mason's face to appear and tell them all what was really going on and what they should do.

Four minutes seemed like an eternity to him as he waited, but finally, the screen lit up, and a spokesman introduced President Mason as if none of them would recognize him when he appeared. He walked to the podium, a stern, serious look on his face. Josh could have been mistaken, but he could swear the man's eyes were filled with a bit of fear as well, and why not? He was human, and every human on the planet was afraid right now.

"My fellow Americans, and loyal employees of the United States, we are all aware of the circumstances which surround today's address. A total of twenty-one unidentified individual alien aircraft have been positioned around the world, six of them in US airspace. In the last day, until very recently, we had not been contacted by the operators of these ships." His eyes flickered. Josh detected the dead giveaway of his untruth. "We can now say we have indeed engaged in communication with them, though obviously not on a face to face basis, nor was it through conventional oral means. We have communicated through encrypted messages sent both ways, and our visitors have not only explained their presence, but they have also clarified what they desire."

He cleared his throat and shifted from one foot to another, barely looking up from the prepared speech which had been placed before him.

"The visitors are indeed aliens and are here from a

planet which our interpreters are unable to put into our language. They are referring to themselves as the 'Oppressors.' That word has been verified with them as being correct." He fell silent for a bit, then cleared his throat and continued. "They fully intend to remain on the planet."

Everyone in the room began to talk all at once, and the overall tone was one of complete panic. Josh was quiet, trying to reason this thing through in his own mind if that was at all possible. His thoughts seemed to make no sense to him, however. Where did they plan to park these ships?

President Mason continued. "The following disclosure is being made only to you at this time. The general public will be briefed once we decide the best course of action regarding the sharing of the information we have. I ask that you do not panic; our greatest strength will be in the peace and calmness which we demonstrate." Now he looked directly into the camera that was aimed at him.

"The Oppressors desire to take up complete inhabitation of Earth. They realize there is no room for them and us, and they have expressed no desire to wipe out humankind. They do, however, want us gone so they can have free access to the planet and its resources. They have prepared a place on another planet, which has not been divulged to us, but they have clarified that the place they have readied will not sufficiently contain every person alive. Therefore, they are saying, they have compiled a battery of very specific tests which everyone will be required to take. These tests, according to them, will determine the strongest and most qualified individuals to be relocated."

The conference room was completely still except for a few scattered sobs coming from women here and there. Josh continued to stare at the screen and tried to make sense of what he was hearing. He was tempted to pinch himself. He had to be dreaming. This couldn't be real.

"We do not plan to give in easily; however, until we are able to determine a solid and effective course of action, we will recommend that everyone maintain the appearance and attitude of cooperation in order to spare their own lives. I know you have questions. I have questions as well, but this is all the information we have at this time. We will be addressing the public with the news and recommendations in a manner conducive to calm. We ask that you keep this information to yourselves, and remain where you are if possible. We will continue to update you as to any progress we make, or any further information we learn. Remember, keep calm. This is the greatest weapon we all have at this time. Thank you."

The screen went immediately dark, and chaos broke out in the room.

R.W.K. Clark

CHAPTER 4

It had been a week since the arrival, and Kamryn was still experiencing shock at what they had learned in the last seven days. No one, as of yet, had laid eyes on any of the Oppressors. While the world had received instructions from them that test sites should be built in each major city area over which their ships hovered, along with directions as to how to build the test sites, Earth's pioneers were told the Oppressors would not touch foot on the ground until testing was ready to begin.

Kamryn was not satisfied to play along.

Five days ago, the day after everyone was made aware of the intentions of the Oppressors, many changes had taken place all over the world. Not only had complete panic spread, but many had been killed by local authorities and the military as they lost their minds. Looting and rape had become commonplace in only one week, and most who really wanted to live had learned to stay inside. From what she could gather, construction had begun on the test sites. Earthlings had been given a time limit; they needed to be complete in one month, which was now only three weeks away.

Kamryn remained on her computer, hacking away as happily as possible, knowing authorities were not paying any attention to her activities. She had determined that she needed to find out as much information as possible about these circumstances. She had no intention of taking any tests.

Melissa had completely flipped out after the initial announcement made by the president. Kamryn had attempted to calm her hysteria, but the girl would have no part of it. Kam had woke the following morning to find herself alone in the small room, and she hadn't seen or heard from Melissa since. Nor had she had any form of communication with any of her other acquaintances. She prided herself on the fact that she had no family or real friends. She would figure this out for herself.

In school, Kamryn had been tagged a genius. She never had to put more than minute effort into her studies, and that usually entailed getting her assignments in on time. She was easily bored; until she got into computers, she had been at the top of the truancy list more often than not. She had full confidence in her ability to not only avoid the testing but to continue to live on her home planet as well.

She had thought and rethought the situation in the last week, barely sleeping and consuming more coffee than anyone had a right to. She knew she was a bit frazzled, but in her mind, it was necessary if she wanted to make it out of this alive and well. Yesterday, she made a firm decision regarding the action she would take. She would bring her most essential belongings; which consisted of her laptop, a few clothes, notebooks, and some personal hygiene items, and she would travel the forty miles to Washington, DC. There she would be able to pursue the proper information, even talking to pertinent people if need be. Wi-Fi would be no problem; when she couldn't tap in for free at a library or coffee house, she would steal it. She would mask her location information when needed. She felt good about her decision. Even if it didn't work the way she wanted, at least she wouldn't be sitting still, feeling as though she were doing nothing to save her own life. So she left.

The world, or at least some of the people in it, were trying to go about life as normally as possible. Busses were running, and many were driving in attempts to escape to… where? She would make it to Washington in less than an hour once she got a ride.

She went to the Interstate 295 entrance located closest to her apartment. Keeping her backpack slung securely over her left arm, she stuck out her right thumb. Within fifteen minutes, a rusty, beat up sedan pulled over, and a dirty, disheveled couple told her to hop in without even asking where she was headed. It was that easy.

Then she was off.

∞

Josh sat in his apartment, smartphone in hand, reading the latest news update regarding the Oppressors and the construction of the testing facilities. He was shaking his head as he read, oblivious to his own actions. He finished and put the phone down on the end table next to the sofa and rubbed his eyes, ignoring the fear in the pit of his stomach. The emotion had become commonplace, not only in his life but in the lives of everyone around him.

He had been pulling full-day shifts for the last week, and this was his first real day off. He had showered as soon as he got home; he smelled like a garbage can full of onion pizza. He intended to sleep but found himself on the damn phone. He needed to take advantage of his time home, and he rose and walked into his bedroom, plopping down onto the bed. They had set up napping facilities at work, and the cots they provided felt like rocks with blankets on them. His mattress felt like heaven.

He lay there thinking about work, tossing and turning. He had been given a highly classified assignment involving writing code that applied to the situation. The government intended to somehow gain access to the information the Oppressors had, while simultaneously blocking our own systems somehow. Josh felt as though he were running in place, and all he could do was go through the motions. He had no idea how to give them what they want, but he was determined. His mind continued to tread through the same mental, work-related waters he had been up to his knees in all week.

Finally, he dozed off, but his sleep was fitful. He awoke a few hours later to discover his blankets knotted around his legs. He was covered in sweat, and he felt the tugging of horror in the pit of his stomach. A nightmare. It slipped away from him before he could recall its details.

He sat up, putting his feet on the floor and his head in his hands. After a moment, he looked at the alarm clock next to his bed. Two-thirty in the afternoon. He had slept for a whole two hours. He thought over his next move. He didn't have to be back to work until morning, but the thought of sitting here doing nothing drove him crazy. He would eat, shower off the sweat, and go back in.

After a microwave dinner consisting of Salisbury steak, runny potatoes, and rubbery corn, he hopped in the shower and got himself together. After dressing, he grabbed his briefcase and headed out the door to his car. The sky overhead was still dark. The hovering ship blocked most of the sun, and all the darkness seemed to do was add to the fear and depression.

Driving with car doors locked was important. Crazy people ran the streets at all times, and when they weren't being arrested, they were being shot down. Carjacking was common, so he double and triple-checked the doors before driving off. The street was amazingly bare of vehicles for this time of the day, but those on foot were everywhere. He checked the locks yet again.

He took a right onto C Street after making sure it was clear. He would be at work in just minutes. He must have been operating on auto-pilot because he didn't see the girl crossing in front of him at all, and when he became fully aware, he had to slam on his brakes to avoid taking her out completely. She froze, her eyes wide and staring directly at him.

He met her eyes and noticed that her face softened when she realized she would not be hit. The bumper of his car appeared to be right against her thigh, but he was really about a foot from her; still, too close for comfort. His heart was pounding with a mixture of fright and relief.

She lifted her hand and flipped him off. He rolled down his window and popped his head out. "I'm so sorry. I guess I wasn't paying attention. Are you okay?"

The girl breathed out a breath that was nearly audible. She nodded and adjusted her backpack. "I'm fine, I guess. You scared me nearly to death!"

"I hope you are really okay." He unlocked his door and got out of the car, not even concerned that this could be a slick carjacking attempt. This girl was beautiful! "Can I give you a ride somewhere? My name is Josh. Josh Nichols."

She studied him carefully, both of them oblivious to the horns sounding behind Josh's car. They were blocking traffic. He realized this and jumping back in he pulled over to the side of the street. She followed him slowly, with a bit of trepidation, keeping her eyes on him the entire time. Cars flew by, curse words streaming from the windows. When had the traffic picked up?

"I can give you a ride? I'm not pressed for time. Where are you going?" He couldn't take his eyes off of her. She wore a calf-length brown peasant skirt and a gauzy cream top which tied at her shoulders. Her shoulders were lightly freckled, as was her nose and cheeks like cinnamon had been sprinkled on her. Her hair was blonde and hung past the middle of her back. She took his breath away.

Her voice brought him back to reality. "I'm Kamryn Reynolds. I would love a ride, but I'm not even sure where I am going. I hiked here from Baltimore, and I've only been in town for a couple of hours trying to figure out what to do next."

"Well, hop in. I'm supposed to be off work until morning, but I was going to go in just to keep myself busy. Are you hungry? We can eat." Josh wasn't hungry, but he would eat if it meant hanging out with this girl.

She looked at her feet, then up and around her. She finally made eye contact. "Actually, I'm starving." She hadn't eaten in days, as a matter of fact.

"Do you want to go someplace in particular? Name it." He kept his eyes on her. He couldn't help himself.

"Well, I guess if it has Wi-Fi, it doesn't matter." She noticed how he looked at her. He seemed harmless enough. She didn't feel that tug in her gut that usually signified trouble. As a matter of fact, she felt completely comfortable, and it surprised her.

Josh scrambled to muster a response. "Well, if you want Wi-Fi, fast food is probably the way to go."

"Thank you. I should tell you that I don't have any money, but…"

"No, please! I've got it. Not a problem." They

walked to the car, and Josh got in first. He unlocked her door, and she got in next to him. Right then a gunshot rang out, and a plate-glass window from a jeweler's place of business seemed to explode. A scream rang out, and a man of about fifty in a business suit ran out the door, blood covering his face. Josh put the car into gear and pressed the pedal to the floor.

As they joined the rest of the traffic, he started a conversation. "Why did you come to DC?" He glanced over at her. She was picking non-existent lint from her brown skirt. She was so cute.

"Um, I guess I was sick of doing nothing to help myself. I wanted to try and find out if there was anything I could do." She didn't want to tell him she was a hacker by trade, and she was here to steal secrets in an effort to survive.

Josh shifted gears. "What do you expect to find?"

She looked at him. "I was hoping to find out if there was anything the government wasn't telling us that would give me a personal upper hand. I don't know, really. Just… something. Anything."

He looked at the road and turned this information over in his mind. How did she intend to get government information? He worked for them, and short of breaking the law the only information they gave him to work with was limited and highly classified. It suddenly occurred to him what she was doing.

"You're hacking, aren't you?" He asked the question with an intentional smile on his face, wanting her to be at ease. It's not like they were going to rush in and arrest her. The feds had much bigger fish to fry at this point in time.

Kamryn got a panic-stricken look on her face. Then the look disappeared instantly. "Why would you think that?"

Josh chuckled. "I work at the Pentagon writing code, and I know only what they want me to know. You would have to hack in to do what you are talking about. It's the only way. Don't worry. Your secret is safe with me."

He took a left, turning in. "Do you want to go in, or drive through?"

"Well, I wanted to set up my laptop," she replied, letting out a breath with relief.

He pulled into a spot and turned off the car. Looking at her made it hard for him to talk, so he only glanced her way now and then. "How about if we play it safe from the criminals and looters. We can drive through, get our food, and go to my place. I have Wi-Fi you can use as long as you promise to use your golden fingers to block my IP address. I know you have tricks I know nothing about, and I'm safe. You are safer with me than you would be on the street trying to do your deeds."

Kamryn smiled at him. A secure place sounded incredible. "I think that's a great idea."

Josh pulled the vehicle out of the spot and drove around to the drive-thru window. They placed their order at the menu board and then pulled on through, paying at the first window and picking up their food at the second one. Within minutes, they were driving the opposite direction on C Street, heading toward his apartment.

CHAPTER 5

Josh led Kamryn into the security building which housed his apartment and after checking his mail, led her to his door. He unlocked it deftly and opened it, reaching inside to the right to turn the light on. He stepped aside so she could enter first, and then he followed, closing the door behind them. He made sure things were locked up tight before he realized the food was still in the back seat of the car.

"Man, I left the food outside! Look, you can set up in here if you like. Help yourself to anything in the fridge to drink. This is the code to the Internet just so you know. I'll be right back." He smiled at her and enjoying the fact that she was here, headed down to get the chicken.

Kamryn took her notebooks and laptop out of her backpack and found an outlet to plug into. Surely the battery would be dead by now so she would take advantage of the opportunity to charge. She plugged her cell in as well, even though she didn't expect to make or receive any calls. Better safe than sorry.

Within minutes Josh was back, locking the door and unpacking the plastic bag of food on the small oak dining table. He had to push paperwork aside to make room. He was obviously a bachelor. The apartment wasn't dirty; it was cleaner than the one-room dive where she had lived in Baltimore. This place just lacked a woman's touch.

While Kamryn worked on the computer, Josh put the food on plates. "Did you grab something to drink?" He asked from the kitchen.

"No. I was pretty focused on getting this up and running. I really appreciate your letting me use your Wi-Fi and hang out here." Her fingers steadily tapped away at the keys as she worked to confuse the signals to avoid detection. Internet service providers and cable companies were some of the easiest systems to hack into if you knew how.

"I have orange juice and Beer, and half a bottle of chardonnay my mom left from Mother's Day. No milk. Oh, and water, of course." He stood at the refrigerator with the door open.

She didn't even look up. "Beer would be great. In a glass, please. Thanks."

Kamryn continued to tap away, even when Josh brought the plate of food and the beer. He walked back to the kitchen for his own, and it wasn't until he had returned and begun to eat that the smell of the chicken got the best of her. Her mouth began to water as she sat there working, and soon she had to find a stopping point and surrender to her ravishing hunger.

She began to eat, taking it slowly because she didn't know how her stomach would handle it. The most

complete meal she had in years, literally, had consisted
of breakfast sandwiches from the Jiffy Mart. She
couldn't remember the last time she had eaten anything
that wasn't on a croissant or English muffin, much less
required a plate. It was hot, and it tasted heavenly. She
wanted it to last, so she pushed every thought of the
present out of her mind, but for the food in front of
her.

Josh pretended to be as engrossed in the sustenance
as she, but he was really watching her out of the corner
of his eye. She was starving! Now that he had gotten a
better look at her here in the apartment, he could see
that she was skin and bones. He supposed hackers
didn't make a regular wage. The thought gave him a
humorless inner laugh.

"How is it?" Speaking to her gave him an excuse to
look directly at her rather than stealing glances.

She finished her bite and wiped her mouth with a
paper napkin. "Wonderful!" Her smile knocked the
wind right out of him, and his heart skipped a beat.

"You don't get to eat much on a hacker's salary, do
you?" As soon as the words were out of his mouth, he
regretted them. 'Hacker' almost seemed like a dirty
word suddenly. She was far too perfect for such a
derogatory term.

She didn't flinch. "No, not really. Can't afford much
of anything." She bit into her chicken thigh, closing her
eyes while she chewed. She was really enjoying the food.

"How did you get into that particular line of
business?" He used as light a voice as possible to keep

the atmosphere pleasant and build trust. She wasn't someone his parents might want him to care to impress, but they were in Iowa, and the world was being invaded by aliens, Who cared?

She looked toward the window at the drawn blinds, seemingly staring into an outside she couldn't see anyway. "I always had a knack for technology and computers. School bored me, and I guess you could say I didn't have much along the lines of parental guidance. It seemed like a great career choice at the time, but after a while, I found myself in a little deeper than I expected. It's not the kind of job you can just quit when you're sick of it, you know?"

"Yeah." He didn't know, but he didn't want the conversation to end now. "So what do you have in mind as far as gathering alien info?"

It was her turn to study him. Could she trust him? Did it even matter anymore?

"Well, I'm not in the bureaucratic mix, but I'm not stupid either. I'm pretty sure Mr. Big living down at 1600 isn't telling the general public everything. For instance, what does this testing consist of? How far along are they on the construction of the testing facilities?" She paused. "I'm not about to just get in line, walk into a gated area, and let them lock it behind me without knowing exactly what I'm doing there. I'm certainly not going to be herded like cattle to the slaughter. What the Oppressors consider human strength may be the opposite of every quality I possess, and I will not let them take my life because they feel I don't measure up." She picked her chicken back up and dug in, biting into a biscuit next.

Josh smiled at the eagerness in which she tore into her food. It did his heart good. He had been starving for intelligent interpersonal communication, and it certainly didn't hurt that Kamryn was a beautiful female specimen.

"Would you like more?" With that, her eyes lit up, and she nodded vigorously.

"I can get it." She rose with her plate and walked over to the dining room table, where she took seconds of chicken, macaroni and cheese, potatoes, and another biscuit. "Do you have another beer?"

He nodded and watched her as she disappeared into the kitchen.

For the next twenty minutes, they ate in silence, but Josh was pondering serious thoughts the entire time. He could help her. He could make the job much easier for her. He worked at the Pentagon, and he wrote code for the United States government. He already knew some of the answers she was looking for. But what if he helped her and found himself in serious trouble? The more he thought about it, the less he thought it was a real possibility. Even if he stood idly by doing nothing, what were the chances he could pass the battery of tests they had outlined to the government?

Finally, he broke the silence. "Kamryn, I want to help. I mean, I think I can help."

She looked at him and studied him closely for a moment. "How can you help me, and why would you want to?"

So he proceeded to tell her what he did for a living. He didn't go into great detail at that point. He wanted to be sure she would listen to what he had to say and accept it. For all he knew she would fear him, fear his position. He wanted to use his words to not only convince her but to put her mind at ease as well.

By the time he was done with his speech, her plate was on the end table next to her chair. Her glass of beer was in her hand, and she stared at him intently in the silence.

"Tell me more," she said quietly.

CHAPTER 6

Andrew Mason emerged from the bathroom drying his hands on a plush white towel. His mind was all over the place. Running a country was a dirty job, he could admit it. But as the old saying goes, someone has to do it.

He re-entered the Oval Office to be greeted by the stares of a few of his best minions. The Secretary of Defense, the head of the Department of Homeland Security and the Vice President. None of whom he liked. All of whom he needed. All he was equipped to do was smile and pass or veto bills. He was a bit of benzoyl on the acne-riddled ass that was America.

Mason walked around his desk, hiked the legs of his tailored dress pants, and took a seat. "Back to our topic, I am hoping to release details of the testing to the public within the next week. Obviously, our concern is that it will trigger more hysteria than we have already experienced from the people. The Oppressors are really putting the pressure on. I get a distinct impression that they consider the people's reaction and the violent behavior they demonstrate to be a test result thus far."

Henry Whitaker, the vice president, spoke. "I feel

the same way. After all, if we kill each other off the Oppressors have fewer tests to administer."

"These are not tests!" This came from the Homeland Security head, Miles James. "None of this has anything to do with testing. It has to do with destroying people and human morale. Let's not blow smoke, gentlemen. It's important we speak frankly if we want to come to any solid conclusions or solutions."

Mason responded, "I would tend to agree. No need to tread lightly or sugarcoat behind these doors."

Carson Wood, the Secretary of Defense, rose to his feet and voiced his standpoint. "I think we should calm down, sit down, and review the demands from start to finish. This is not something that we can cover one time and make a firm decision on as to which way to go."

"Carson, I completely agree. Speaking from my point of view, I'd have to say that I need a bit more coverage. Final word." Mason sat down heavily at his desk, letting out a sigh as he did so. He ran his hand through what little brown hair he had left. It really boiled down to just stroking his scalp.

The four men settled in with their files before Miles spoke up, "The very first communique from the Oppressors consisted of introduction. It seemed cordial enough, letting us know who they were, where they came from, and why they were here."

"Resources," said Whitaker flatly.

Miles James replied with a matter of fact, "Exactly."

"With this in mind, and based on the fact that we have now been personally introduced, the Oppressors begin to present us with their demands. They don't call them demands, however. Stipulations, I believe, is the best word we have for it." James glanced down at his file, then directed his eyes back to the three men before him. "Do you want to cover the individual demands one by one?"

President Mason stared straight ahead for a moment before nodding blankly and voicing his decision. "Absolutely. The more informed, the more prepared," he replied.

Miles took a deep breath and proceeded:

"I will relay them to you in the same manner in which they have literally been interpreted to us through our people, our interpretive officials.

"Number One: We are here to sustain the lives of the people of our race through the use of a countless number of resources located on your planet.

"Number Two: We have no interest in the elimination of your species by means of force. It is our sincere interest to allow your species to procreate and continue its cycle of life, but on a limited, and controlled, basis.

"Number Three: The individuals allowed to continue species life will be determined in accordance with their strength in all aspects of the lives we have observed. This includes intelligence, moral values, reasoning, determination, and physical strength.

"Number Four: The tests which have been prepared for you are incremented by these strengths. Each strength will be tested as we see fit to determine the most ideal individuals who exhibit the highest combinations of the strengths.

"Number Five: Those we do not deem fit after the tests are complete, will be terminated.

"This was the second part of the communique delivered to us by the Oppressors." Miles James kept his eyes on his manila folder, closing it, yet keeping his forefinger in the place he left off.

All men in the room paused to consider, letting the words James had just spoken sink in. This was vital to making the correct, and best, decision for the people of the United States, and essentially, the world.

After what seemed like hours, Andrew Mason raised his head. "From what we have just reviewed, from where we are now, what do you think men?"

At first, there was dead silence. None of the men made eye contact with each other, and the tension in the office was tangible. Regardless of how many times they covered this information, it never seemed to get any easier to stomach.

Carson Wood cleared his throat and shifted uncomfortably in his chair. "What can we think? Let's just continue and discuss any new ideas when we're finished. So far none of us has experienced a light bulb over their head which will make any kind of difference. Just continue."

Miles went on. "The Oppressors have given us clear instructions regarding the areas which will house the testing facilities. Here in the States, this includes Chicago, Illinois; Nome, Alaska; Washington, DC;

Seattle Washington; San Antonio, Texas; Sacramento, California; Honolulu, Hawaii; Miami, Florida; and finally, Denver, Colorado. Nine facilities total, and each will take test participants from a preset area for which the facility serves as a hub. Initially we believed them to demand the construction of six facilities, and we made the people aware of such; however, this number was incorrect, and our interpreters made the distinction as they became more in tune with the language spoken by the Oppressors. There are, as we know, only six enemy ships in American airspace." He finally looked up from his clipboard, which was really useless to him. He had all but memorized these documents in recent days.

It was Whitaker's turn to speak. "Let's cover how the people are to arrive at their prospective facility, and what we are all to expect regarding testing."

"We will all go to the facility within closest proximity to our state of residence. We will all be required to pre-register in accordance to our census records, and anyone found missing is to be sought out, pursued, and taken to the correct facility by authorities. If they refuse or fight, they are to be terminated." Miles paused long enough to take a sip of water from a glass next to him. "Existing authorities on all levels are to be tested last, as they are needed to fulfill this portion of the demands."

President Mason spoke up. "The tests themselves, consist of individual strength tests. Some, such as the intellectual and scholastic testing, will be primarily written. Others, like strength and survival, will be physical in nature. Tests for bravery and fighting skill will actually consist of combat situations between testees."

"The only thing truly unclear is what the Oppressors consider 'passing.' We have attempted to clarify this point with them. Will the smartest and strongest be granted a spot on the new planet? Or will the weakest, or those who present less of a threat to the aliens and their agenda? These questions have gone ignored by the Oppressors to this point," stated Miles James. These words sparked another stretch of silence as the men contemplated the facts yet again.

Finally, Henry Whitaker spoke up. "If they gave us an answer to that question, it would cause even more pandemonium than we have already. Those who are even halfway intelligent, strong, or successful know it. What would that mean for the world in the next few weeks? The weak would run and hide, and mass suicide would likely be the result. It certainly seems like a no-win situation. Unless, of course, we attack."

This observation had been voiced countless times, but the Oppressors' ships were massive, and nothing on Earth compared when it came to deciding what would be used to combat these unseen enemies.

All four men simply nodded their heads and continued to consider the facts.

Finally, Andrew Mason spoke, breaking the silence. "Take it from the top, Miles."

CHAPTER 7

Josh Nichols walked from the elevator to his office the morning after meeting (and feeding) Kamryn Reynolds. He never made it to the office yesterday afternoon as intended. Rather, he and Kamryn had sat up late into the night talking. He had put a huge amount of classified information on the table, including facility and testing specifics which the general public had no idea about. Kamryn had become extremely sober during the duration of their conversation, even presenting him with a theory he had not considered: what if the weak or stupid were the ones to pass?

The very idea of this was petrifying, and he had carried a sick, heavy feeling in the pit of his stomach ever since. What if that were so? He had just assumed that the best of them would be granted the right to exist, but her argument had been solid. The Oppressors would want to ensure their mission was a success, and what better way to do that than to kill off the strongest and smartest on the planet?

She had also asked him about any plans to fight back. Josh knew there were none, and not because they didn't want to. They simply had no idea how to go about it. While the powers that be were constantly working on a solution to this issue, they found that their limited knowledge of the Oppressors themselves, as well as their hovering ships, hindered them greatly. In the very beginning, when the ships first came, the military had indeed attempted to strike, but the puny aircraft being used could not administer the power needed to do more than reveal unseen force fields around each and every one of the Oppressors' craft. This had led to the standstill they were all living with.

Kamryn had come up with a plan on a very small scale. She wanted to attempt to get into the computers on the ships if that was indeed what they even were. For all Josh knew, those things were operated by mind control. They had no idea how advanced these beings were, or even what they looked like. Kamryn had been insistent that this was the next logical step. She asked, no, begged, Josh to continue to divulge any information, no matter how seemingly unimportant, to her. Anything he could get his ears and eyes on. He agreed. After all, it looked like it wasn't going to matter in the end, anyway, and he didn't want to take any of this lying down.

He entered his office and plopped down at his desk, booting up his system. He logged on so he could get to work, and opened the desk's file drawer to take out the code he had been working on when he had gone home two days ago. There was a sharp knock on his door, and Gladys Emerson, one of the numerous secretaries in their unit, entered.

"Good morning, Josh. Peter Wells wanted me to get

this to you as soon as you got in. He said to put any work which you are focusing on the back burner. This takes priority." Peter Wells was the head of the entire unit, but first and foremost, he was involved in the country's Internet security.

"What is it, Gladys? Any ideas?"

She just shook her head. "Of course not. I'm a peon around here, Josh. You know that." She smiled grimly, nodded, and left the office.

She had handed him a large yellow envelope, marked Classified, of course. It was very heavy and very thick. He was just preparing to break the seal when the intercom on his phone buzzed loudly, making him nearly jump out of his chair.

"Josh, this is Pete Wells. Did Gladys bring you an envelope this morning?"

"Yes, she did. She just left. I was getting ready to give it a gander and get started."

Peter replied, "Hold that thought. Bring it to my office and let's have a meet. See you in five?" The intercom went dead immediately.

Josh loved the curtness exhibited by those in charge. His head was swimming. He had never had a meet or even bumped into Peter Wells in the halls. This was serious indeed. Josh was just a lowly code writer, the youngest of all in the department. He felt as if he was just a step up from Gladys, the Peon.

He grabbed a pen out of the cup on his desk, a fresh legal pad, and with the envelope in hand, he made his way to the elevator. He felt butterflies in his stomach, as though his professional future depended on this meeting, but he knew that was silly. He was pretty sure he wouldn't be getting a promotion any time soon.

He arrived at Wells' office and told the boss's secretary he was there.

"He's expecting you. I wouldn't even have a seat. Just follow me, Mr. Nichols." She was cute and curvy, with long blonde hair and too much make-up, but her rear end swing could catch the eye of a blind man. He enjoyed the view, but she wasn't his type. Leave all the plastic for Barbie and Ken.

"Mr. Wells, Mr. Nichols." She held the door open and stood aside so Josh could enter. She smiled a tight smile and shut the door tightly as she left.

"Have a seat, Josh. We have a lot to cover and very little time. We need you to get started." Josh took a chair directly across from Wells and settled his things on a small table next to it.

"As you know, testing facilities are being constructed diligently, and testing is expected to begin in a few short weeks. You were off yesterday so you may not be aware that President Mason and his group met extensively yesterday to pick each other's brains regarding any course of action which may potentially save humanity. They have some ideas which require your expertise if they are to even be considered. I want you to know you are our top code writer, and we think your education and experience is exceptional. The first thing you should know is that the Oppressors will be setting foot on Earth sometime in the next couple of weeks to inspect the facilities. They have made us aware that they want them done before the deadline given prior. They seem to be getting a bit edgy. They have also made us aware that they will be helping with the herding process."

He stopped speaking to let that information sink in. It did, and it was horrifying. Now, all of this seemed much more real than ever before. Indeed, this was really happening.

"Can't we simply attack when they come off the ships?" To Josh, this seemed like the obvious solution.

Wells shook his head. "It's not that simple. For one thing, we have no idea how many are aboard each craft. We do not know about their weapons, their physical make-up, nothing. We have no idea what they are capable of morally or technologically.

"What we need you to do is get familiar with the material in the packet. We need a very specific code. What you are able to produce will make or break us when it comes to familiarizing ourselves as much as possible with who and what we are really dealing with, including their craft." This was beginning to sound a lot like the ideas Kamryn had put on the table, minus the actual 'hacking,' of course. But that is what it boiled down to.

"We have had innumerable men and women attempting what we are asking you to do, to no avail. We are hoping you can produce. We have only a couple of weeks, maybe less if they change their minds about the timeline again." Then he finally said the word. "We even have top-of-the-line hackers, the best. They are making little to no progress."

Josh's eyes grew wide. "I'm not a hacker, Mr. Wells. I wouldn't even know where to begin!" Nothing like failing before you even get started.

"No time like the present, Josh," said Wells grimly.

Josh stared down at his hands, barely noting the severe tremor. He had Kamryn, of course, but he would never be able to get the classified documents home for her to study. He was at a loss.

Suddenly he spoke. "I know someone."

"What do you mean, you know someone?" Josh had Wells' full attention.

He took a deep breath and mustered his courage. Did it really matter if he got himself into trouble? Maybe not, but he couldn't get Kamryn into trouble. He would tread lightly. "I know a hacker. Someone who has been doing it professionally. For a number of years."

"What kind of education and background does this individual have? How do you know they are any good?" Josh could detect a bit of desperation in his voice. He had likely not meant for that to be heard, but Josh ran with it anyway.

"I will tell you that this individual has extensive experience, and their abilities are impressive." He really had no idea how impressive Kamryn's abilities were, but this was the perfect opportunity for her to get her hands on the information she wanted, all while focusing on her personal plan, which seemed to fall directly into line with theirs.

Wells considered his words for a moment, then asked, "What are you doing working for the government and having associations with such an individual? Hell, it doesn't even matter, now does it?"

Josh shook his head in response. "Not really."

Peter Wells thought for a few more seconds, staring at a set of perpetual swinging silver balls on his desk. He looked into Josh's eyes. "I'll tell you what. Take the packet to your office and start to give it a good going over. I will call my people right away. At this point, we are all ready to go to any extreme in hopes it will work. We need to come up with something." He looked back at the silver balls, then back at Josh. "Don't get too comfortable. I will likely be calling you back up here very shortly. I don't know this person, or if they are any good, but the fact of the matter is, we have nothing to lose."

"No problem. I'll get right on this and get a feel for what you need me to do. I'll be waiting for your call." Josh rose from his chair and gathered the envelope, tablet, and pen. Wells also stood, coming around the desk to walk him out the door.

"Thanks, Nichols. Talk to you soon." He guided Josh out of his office with a hand on his elbow, shutting the door gently behind him.

Back in his office, he sat at his desk, staring in disbelief at the blank wall in front of him. He wanted to call Kamryn but decided to wait until Wells called him back. After about ten minutes of uncontrolled thought, he picked up the envelope, broke the seal and began to read.

Forty-five minutes flew by before Josh looked up from the stack before him. He let out a long, ragged breath. Home Land Security knew so much more than they were telling. Of course, did anyone expect the full truth from the world's governing parties? No, but the fact was that half the things they did reveal were lies. With less than two weeks before the Oppressors set foot on the earth's soil to begin the herding process. Wells had lied to his face knowing he would soon know the truth. The only consolation to all of this was the fact that, as an employee of the government, he would be in with some of the last being herded.

He thought about Kamryn. So smart, so beautiful. Kamryn. Now it seemed more important than before to get her foot in the door here. He didn't know her at all, but he certainly wanted to. That wouldn't happen if…

The buzzer on his intercom startled him back to reality. "Nichols, Wells here. I need to see you in my office right away."

He was not even done speaking and Josh was heading out his office door to see Wells.

CHAPTER 8

"Thanks for getting back up here so quickly. Have a seat, Nichols." Wells gestured to the chair Josh had been sitting in less than an hour ago.

He sat quickly, his eyes glued to Peter Wells' face. He was completely unreadable, and this made Josh feel edgy and unsettled. Certainly, he wouldn't have called him all the way back to his office with news that was negative.

Wells began. "Well, this is very out of the ordinary for the United States government, as you likely know well. But so are the circumstances the world finds itself in right now. Traditionally, we would accept no one as an employee without a thorough background check and intensive training for the position which they are being considered. Have you begun reading through the classified information?"

Josh felt anger rise up into his throat, but he reined it in and nodded.

"Good. Then you are beginning to get a much firmer grasp on the dire nature of our situation. Sorry for the 'untruths' I spoke earlier. I had to tread lightly, and watching your responses and expressions is all a very serious part of that. Now, as for your friend. I spoke with my supervisor, and the two of us had a brief but to the point telephone conference with President Mason and his men. They feel pretty much the same way about giving this person a shot as I do: what have we got to lose?"

Josh continued to listen and watch his expressions. It didn't matter what this guy ever said to him from here on out. He would never believe anything that came out of his mouth again. All he knew was if they were going to give Kamryn a shot at hacking the Oppressors' ships, he was all for it.

"So what do you want me to do?" Josh tried to give the appearance of calmness, but he knew that Kamryn would be more than ecstatic at this opportunity.

"Well, it's obviously priority that you get this person in here yesterday. We will forego the formal procedures for hiring, and if your friend is successful, we may consider keeping him or her after the crisis has passed. Is this a man or a woman?" Wells waited expectantly for the answer.

"She is a woman, and she has been doing this for a long time. She encountered a bit of trouble in Baltimore recently for her activities, but I really don't know the details. What I do know is that we have spoken extensively about the Oppressors, and she has a very good base plan. She wants to hack directly into their ships, but she needs to get her hands on as much true information as possible. I can't tell you the details. I don't know them," Josh replied.

Wells nodded. "Then we are her people. Can you call her and get her to come right away? We can meet, the three of us, along with my supervisor, and we can find out what she needs, after we get a rundown on her ideas, of course."

"Well, she doesn't drive right now, and she is very new to the area." Like two days new, Josh thought to himself. "I would likely have to go fetch her in my car."

Wells nodded again. He was starting to remind Josh of a bobblehead. "Get to it, then. As soon as the two of you get back, bring the classified information I supplied you with and come directly up here. I will be waiting. Oh, and call me on your cell when you are on the way back so I can have Matt Johnson in here waiting when you arrive." He fished around in his desk drawer, finally pulling a half-used pad of sticky notes out. He jotted something on one of them, peeled it back, and held it out for Josh to take.

"My cell number. Now, hurry up. I will be waiting."

Josh rose, sticky note in hand, and walked out the door. He took the elevator to his office and grabbed the envelope, put it into his briefcase. He then made a beeline for the main entrance.

Twenty minutes later, he was sitting in his apartment giving Kamryn a quick rundown on the situation as she tied her sneakers and put her laptop in her backpack. Her eyes were lit up with excitement.

"I just can't believe you literally got me in the door!" She was smiling from ear to ear.

Josh shook his head. "It only worked because they

need someone to hack, and none of their people are having any success." He handed her the classified envelope, which he had pulled from his briefcase on his way in. "You will need to begin to go over this while we drive back. I hope you are as good as you say."

"I never said I was good, Josh. I don't have to. I know I am."

He smiled at her. Her confidence was very sexy, and she looked more beautiful to him than ever. No time for that though. Time to think clearly.

"Ready? We need to get back ASAP." She gave him a quick nod and followed him out the door.

During the drive back, Josh phoned Wells and let him know they were on their way in, and within a half hour, they were back at the Pentagon, seated in Wells' office with him, Matt Johnson, and another man Josh had never seen before.

"Mr. Wells, this is Kamryn Reynolds. Kamryn, Mr. Wells, my supervisor. This gentleman is Matt Johnson, and I'm not sure who this is." Josh motioned to the stranger.

Wells did the bobblehead. "Josh, Kamryn, this is Miles James, Director of Homeland Security. He will be heading the project and acting directly on behalf of President Mason. Before we get started, can I offer you something to drink? We will likely be meeting for a couple of hours."

"I'd like coffee, black please." Kamryn put her backpack on the floor and sat in the chair closest to her, as did Josh. The three men all sat, Wells pressing the button on his intercom as he did.

"Sharon, I need a carafe of coffee and the works, please. Five cups." He let go of the button before Sharon could respond. "Kamryn, could you briefly fill us in on what you do?"

"Well," she replied, searching for the most diplomatic words possible. "I'm a hacker."

Bobble Head did it again. "We know you are a hacker. Tell us whose computers, in general, you have hacked. There really is no need to be specific, and there will be no repercussions."

For the next ten or fifteen minutes, Kamryn gave the men a quick overview. She had not only hacked into the systems of some major corporate conglomerates, but she had also succeeded in doing the same to three well-known universities and a couple of government systems. It was the government systems which got her busted, she explained, as she had managed to issue herself large refund checks. She succeeded three years running, getting away with a very large amount of money before they caught up with her. Josh felt admiration swell in his chest.

The universities she hacked into as paid jobs for rich students who were failing their courses. The others, she stated, she just did for fun and practice.

"I'm supposed to be attending a court date in Baltimore at the federal courthouse next month, but I'm kind of hoping you guys can make this disappear if I can help you like you need me to."

Miles James spoke up. "So what makes you think

you can actually breach the Oppressors' systems if indeed they exist?"

"I know they exist; I discovered a signal today while I was working before I came in. It is a strange one, but it is there nonetheless, and if it is there, I can breach it. I promise you." The look on Kamryn's face was set and serious. She had full confidence in herself and her abilities, and she meant every word she spoke. "I realize I am dealing with a very limited time frame, but given the life and death set of circumstances before us all, as well as the fact that I love what I do, I will commit as much time as is needed until I succeed. Josh tells me I have just under two weeks. I believe I'm just who you are looking for."

It was Matt Johnson's turn to speak. "Would the two of you excuse us while we confer? You can step just outside the door. We will be back with you shortly."

As if on cue, Sharon entered the office with the coffee. "Sharon, these two are going to join you in the outer office for a brief moment. Take care of them, please."

Sharon smiled with her blood red lips. "Absolutely. Come with me, please."

Josh and Kamryn took a seat on a leather couch which sat against a wall in the outer office. "What do you think? Did I do okay?" Her nervousness was much more obvious now that they were basically alone.

"You did perfectly. I don't think it's a matter of should they use you. It's past that now, Kam." Josh offered her a comforting smile. This was not about getting a good job. It was about survival.

Only minutes had passed before Sharon's intercom buzzed. "Send them back in, please." She rose from her desk and motioned to the office door.

"We can see ourselves in, thank you," Josh told her. They entered the office and took the same chairs as before.

Wells began, "As you may have guessed, we are anxious to see what you can do for us. Josh will write any code you need. I made a call and as we speak a bigger office is being prepared for you two to share. Josh, your computer and entire desk will be relocated. Are things secure down there?"

"Yes. I locked it up before leaving to get her," he replied.

"Good. You will be on the same floor, but you will be moving into Tom Gray's old space." Josh smiled. That was a kick-ass office. "The first order of business will be to soak up as much of the information we give you as possible. Sharon will get you a code to log onto the government system, and she will do it as you leave. Go directly down and get busy reviewing the information I have already supplied you with. The files on the computer you will need are all under 'Operation Native.' If you discover you need anything extra, just ask. Within reason, of course."

Both Kamryn and Josh nodded. It seemed to be catching around this place. She looked over at Josh. "I'm ready if you are." Her eyes were on fire, and he could tell she could barely contain herself.

"Ready," he said. They stood and made their way to the door.

"Sharon, I will need login information and identification for Kamryn Reynolds. Is that with a 'C,' Kamryn?" Wells was looking at her expectantly when she turned to face him.

"No. K-A-M-R-Y-N. Reynolds is just Reynolds." Both waited until he motioned for them to leave before heading out.

"And Kamryn, thank you for serving your country… or the world, I should say." Miles James looked very serious.

Kam responded, "No, thank you. Nothing will please me more than to get rid of the Oppressors. Nothing."

Before heading to the new office, Josh and Kamryn stopped in his tiny old hole-in-the-wall. He grabbed the legal tablet and the same pen he had earlier that morning, and as they were leaving to go to the new space, the workers who were moving them entered.

"We will be in the new office," Josh told them.

In minutes, they found themselves seated, Kamryn at the desk supplied for her use, and Josh on the floor, cross-legged. She pulled the classified file out of her backpack and began to review, using the tablet Josh brought to jot notes on. In five minutes his desk, chair, and files arrived, and he was able to make himself comfortable also while they got his computer set up. She could not log in on her own until she received her credentials.

They began going through the classified file together, a page at a time. At around ten in the morning, Kamryn got her log in code and other credentials. She had stepped out with Sharon briefly to have her photo taken. Now it was nearly three in the afternoon. Josh went to grab a late lunch, leaving her there to continue working.

The things she learned from the paper documents alone were enough to run her blood cold. She discovered that the Oppressors had not only laid out strict demands on the people of Earth, they also threatened complete destruction of the entire planet and all of its inhabitants in one fell swoop if their demands were not followed to a tee. In addition to taking over for the sake of the world's resources, they fully intended to take up residence here. They claimed every ship that had arrived held the full number of their people.

The planet they came from was laid waste as a direct result of their scavenger activities, not a living soul remaining on it. The planet they offered to relocate Earth's people to, possessed just enough of what was needed in terms of atmosphere, as well as minimal resources, to sustain life, but only for a fraction of those who lived here presently.

Why not just wipe us out? She wondered this to herself and no sooner did the thought cross her mind that she came across the answer. They did not consider themselves to be cold-blooded thieves and murderers. They actually took great pride in what they considered to be a high level of mercy. They seemed, from what she read, to truly believe this about themselves.

Kamryn came to a single cold, hard conclusion: kill or be killed. It was as simple as that.

They would set foot on terra firma in just under two weeks. This fact did not frighten her. She believed in herself, and while she didn't believe a thing the world's officials said, she did believe each and every one of them wanted to live. This was a fact that was in her favor. They would do what it took to help, particularly if she could show consistent progress.

Kamryn could find nothing in the file which clarified anything regarding the Oppressors' ships or method of computing. The guys upstairs had told her they had hackers working around the clock. What were the idiots doing, anyway? She had discovered an unidentified signal from the comfort of Josh's apartment. This did not make sense to her, and she concluded they were testing her to find out what her abilities were. Lies; always lies.

Josh returned with two green salads and some packaged dressings, as well as two iced teas. Kamryn had already logged on to her computer using her passcode, and she had already opened up the Project Native file. Her main objective was to locate anything she could which discussed the computer system being used by the ships.

She didn't have to look far. The government knew they used an advanced method of computing, and they believed the ships' mechanisms were dependent on it. The issue had never been not knowing because they did know. One bright hacker had discovered this early on. The real problem was figuring it out, and this had proven to be the obstacle for every ivy league computer genius the government had assigned to do the job.

"Take a break, Kamryn. Get a quick bite," Josh suggested. Suddenly her mouth began to water, and she turned herself reluctantly from her screen.

She chose ranch dressing, and as she squeezed the white goo out of its packet, she spoke quietly. "They have known about the ships' computers pretty much all along. They just hit a brick wall. The fools couldn't go any further."

She let that sink in as she took a hefty bite of her salad and chewed it, looking at his face to read his expressions.

"What do you mean, they knew?"

She nodded. "They knew since almost the beginning. I'm not going to get mad about it. I am going to crack the son of a bitch wide open." She was calm and confident, and this helped him to feel the same way.

"Then that is exactly what you should do," Josh replied.

R.W.K. Clark

CHAPTER 9

Over the next thirteen days, things began to change quickly. Kamryn was able to make rapid progress identifying the language of the system used by the Oppressors. It was digital—and though it was foreign—she was able to easily learn and adapt. This enabled her to show progress to authorities when she was asked. Josh busied himself with any code she needed to be written, and by the time they had been at it for ten days, she was sure she knew enough for those upstairs and at the White House to begin formulating a solid plan of action.

She had one of her own. She wanted to disable any weapons they had, as well as the force fields around the ships, which would allow the military to effectively attack. She kept steady notes of these things, and reported them diligently, along with any other ideas the two had.

True to form, the Oppressors set foot on Earth a full day ahead of schedule. It was a horrifying thing to witness, and chaos had once again been sparked the world over. As they hoped, she was sure. Spreading panic seemed to be the aliens' favorite weapon.

On the day before they emerged, President Mason held a State of the Union address to inform the people of the Oppressors' intent to reveal themselves a day early. They would begin the herding process after addressing the world themselves. How this would be done was anyone's guess.

Fear and hysteria were universal reactions, the biggest fear being based on the tentative appearance, and potential level of aggression, of the unknown aliens. Countless suicides took place, and many people seemed to simply disappear off the face of the earth. It was presumed they went into hiding.

Before the 'unveiling' of the Oppressors, a meeting was held which included the attendance of both Kamryn and Josh, as well as the president's team, Peter Wells, and his own supervisor, Matt Johnson. Because of the progress, the two made regarding the interpretation of the ships' computer system, and the additional revelations they were bringing to light concerning how the Oppressors knew so much about human life on Earth, the Project Native discovery team now consisted only of them.

"Josh, Kamryn. We are pretty much down to Zero Hour now, as you are well aware. While we have been told by the Oppressors that those in specific authoritative and government positions would be last to be herded, we also realize their capacity for deception. It is more important now than ever that your focus remains steady on bringing down their ships' defenses." This was President Mason, and while he maintained a calm façade, the look in his eyes spoke volumes more about the fear he felt. "We need you to remain here at all times, working steadily toward the accomplishment of this goal."

Josh replied, "Well, you should know that we are prepared for that, and have been. Since we are here ninety-nine percent of the time, we have clothing, and we have been showering in the gym facilities on grounds anyway. Slacking hasn't been an acceptable option."

Kamryn interjected, "We are closer than ever before to breaking down the code they use to control the ships, and as you know, we have also uncovered a few of the methods they have used to basically hack into our systems. These methods are what has enabled them to gain the in-depth education they needed regarding humans, and thus allowed them to catch us unaware and keep their grip on us."

"Fill me in a bit more on this. I understood you had more information about how they were able to gain understanding regarding Earth and humankind, but I need a firmer grasp on what you know," said President Mason.

Kamryn proceeded to fill in the gaps for the Commander-in-Chief. Not only had the Oppressors gained free access to all data on the planet through the computers, but they also seemed to have some type of ability, through their system, to track what people were doing and saying at the time it was being done. She emphasized the importance of keeping words at a minimum, explaining that Josh and she had developed a method of communication which had likely thrown a wrench into their works.

"Eliminate obvious words; use more gestures. Keep things at a minimum," she made eye contact with each man in the room one at a time as she spoke. "The reason progress has been so slow for us, I believe, is that they have been onto us the entire time. This allowed them to change things up as they pleased, and this is precisely what they have done." She stopped there.

Heads nodded all around. Carson Wood, the Secretary of Defense, spoke up. "Should we resort to…" he proceeded to pretend to write on a non-existent pad with an invisible pen.

"If the conversation applies to our plans, absolutely." She needed them to understand that the Oppressors knew more than humans understood. She was firm in this belief.

The Oppressors were due to emerge from their ships at eight o'clock Eastern Standard Time the next morning. Josh knew that he and Kamryn had a lot of work to do in preparation for this, the first item consisting of shutting down their ability to get inside of Earth's systems. He had constructed a very powerful firewall with hopes of protecting Kamryn's hacking activities from detection. So far it seemed to be working, but they didn't know if it would last, or even if it really was working. They were going on a wing and a prayer, so every second they had was vital to the mission.

When the meeting was over, Josh and Kam made their way back down to their office. They rode the elevator in silence, but Josh had his eyes on her the entire time. He knew he was in love with her; how could he not be? She was beautiful, smart, and in his eyes, accomplished. What she was doing was not only admirable, it was amazing, and she was getting the job done.

They got to the office and went directly about their business, keeping conversation to a minimum. For the next two hours, she focused on the defense and offense systems of the ships. She was sure they not only possessed weapons meant for the killing of one individual at a time, from what she could see, but each ship also had a single missile type weapon. While she had a difficult time determining its power, she was sure one shot could completely wipe out each of the cities which the ships were positioned over, if need be. This would mean the destruction of the planet and all of its inhabitants if they were used together. They needed to tread very lightly.

Once she was able to communicate this news, she wrote it out on paper for Josh. As he read his eyes grew larger. When he was finished, he looked at her and simply nodded his understanding. He was not going to speak any words.

She knew that the first order of business would be to shut their systems completely down, which would render all weapons and force fields powerless, and that is what she wrote to him next. Turning back to the computer she got to work trying to come up with the best plan of cyber-attack for the job.

By eleven that morning, she made a major breakthrough. She was able to actually identify the general point of origin of their computer signal. While she could not specify exactly where it was coming from, she now knew it was there with certainty. This could be just what they were looking for. To block this somehow would give them the upper hand they so desperately needed. The question was how?

When she discovered this, Josh was getting lunch for them both. She wanted to tell him and began to pace the floor anxiously, thinking hard about the new information until he returned. This was exactly the kind of job he was needed for.

Josh strolled into the office with food and drink in hand. Kam stopped pacing and looked up at him with a broad smile on her face.

"What?" He asked.

She chose her words carefully. "I found something big."

He looked confused, but she held her finger to her lips in a gesture of silence. She motioned for him to come over to her desk. He put down the food and sat in his chair, rolling it until he was next to her. She wrote, as briefly as possible, what she had found, and they both stood, jumping up and down, arms in the air until their actions culminated in a huge hug.

She could smell his skin and his hair, and suddenly

she was hit with the reality of her feelings for this man. He had always been obviously good looking, but his smell now incited her to be aware of the contours of his body, the tautness of his muscles, and she subconsciously found herself pressing her body against his.

They both jerked apart, blushing and flustered. She knew her face was red, and keeping her eyes to the ground, said, "We need to see Wells right away."

"Let's go up," he responded. She grabbed the tablet and pen, and he did the same with another legal pad from his desk. As they walked out of the office, he took her hand. She looked him in the eyes and smiled shyly.

She could sure use another of those hugs, and much, much more.

R.W.K. Clark

CHAPTER 10

Wells was out to lunch, so they decided to wait on him. They really couldn't proceed without giving him a heads-up and getting his input. He would need to talk to President Mason's team somehow and find out how they wanted her and Josh to move forward. Things would have to be lined up if they were going to try to shut out the alien signal. It would be pointless without having a plan of attack established.

Peter Wells returned at one-thirty, and seeing the looks on both of their faces as they sat on the leather sofa was enough for him.

"Come on in," he said, and they jumped up and followed him into his inner sanctum.

As soon as they were seated, Kamryn put her finger to her lips in what was becoming an all too familiar sign to exercise verbal discretion. Wells nodded, holding her eyes as he did so. She handed the same piece of paper to him across the desk which she had written for Josh explaining what she had found.

He read it silently. When he was finished, he looked up at her, his eyes betraying his excitement.

"And?" He asked.

She put her pen and paper to use, writing, "We need to confer with the other powers. We need to determine a specific signal blocking method, and we need to have an attack strategy in place. I have ideas regarding the blocking, but I need to know what resources are at my disposal so I can develop something effective."

She turned that note over to Wells, and they both waited impatiently for him to read it. He looked up at them, resting his chin on his fist. He was thinking hard. Finally, he picked up the phone and punched in a few numbers. After a moment, he spoke.

"Matt, Peter here. We need to reconvene as soon as possible. Good. You make the calls. See you soon." He hung up the phone and sat back in his chair, fingers laced behind his head. "Nice job, Kamryn."

She finally spoke. "Do we have access to an old school overhead projector, by chance? It would make the meeting go a lot more smoothly if we did."

"Excellent!" He pushed his intercom button and said, "Sharon, get maintenance to bring a working overhead projector up from storage stat."

"Yes, sir."

Josh asked, "Should we come back when they get here? I mean, there really is nothing we can do until we confer."

"No, no, no. Stay here. Make small talk. Maybe it will… you know… cause a distraction," replied Wells. "So, what did you two have for lunch?"

They all burst out in laughter, mostly from the tension, but also from relief. "To be honest, our lunch is sitting on my desk in my office. I had just returned when she shared her good news," Josh replied.

"Well, we can't have that. Run down and grab it. You can eat while we wait. I had prime rib at Morton's; simply dynamite, but I likely gained five pounds. Good thing the wife likes me thick."

Josh smiled. "I could eat, and I'm sure this wisp of a girl needs to. I'll be back in a flash." He rose and left the office feeling light on his feet.

When he was gone, Kamryn looked at Wells awkwardly. She had never done as well alone with strange men as she did with a monitor and keyboard.

"You two are hitting it off nicely, I'd say." Wells was grinning at her like a father might a daughter who he had accepted as grown.

She felt the blood rush into her cheeks once again. "I don't know…" She trailed off, embarrassed by the question.

"No need to flush. I can see it. If I may speak freely, I think you two make a heck of a team." He was smiling slightly in an effort to make her more comfortable. They were all under extreme pressure, and this young girl had the full weight of it. "How old are you, Kamryn?"

She replied, "Twenty-three."

Wells chuckled and then shook his head for a change. "Despite all this, you're human. It's okay. If everything works out, you might be surprised at the future potential the two of you have."

She smiled again and allowed herself to entertain the thought that everything just might work out. What would it be like to be with Josh? She was more than afraid to hope.

"You know, Kamryn, if this plays out you are going to be a hero." He looked at her seriously. "Contemplate the weight of what you are doing. It's huge, young lady."

She nodded and shifted in her seat. She wanted to live, of course. Having a future would be great. The fact was she had no idea how to make that dream become a reality, at least not yet.

Josh was back sooner than they thought, and she was relieved. She felt her smile spread across her face when he came into the office, and she took great pleasure in the fact that hers were the first eyes his sought out. He smiled back.

He was so proud of her, of what she was doing. He couldn't believe he had been lucky enough to be the one to almost take her out with his car. He wanted to get her alone badly and show her how he felt. He wouldn't be any good saying it.

The two ate while Wells spoke of his grandchildren, wife, and the house they were buying in the Hamptons. His eyes lit up when he talked about Mrs. Wells. You could see he loved her deeply and fretted terribly over the welfare of his family at this time.

Before the food was gone, the men began to shuffle in. President Mason and Carson Wood were first. Within minutes Matt Johnson followed suit, and seconds later Henry Whitaker, accompanied by the skittish Miles James, entered as well.

Wells began. "Gentlemen, we're waiting on an overhead projector." With that thought, he buzzed Sharon. "Where is my hardware, Sharon? What's going on?"

"Maintenance is here now, sir. Be right in." Sharon sounded very tense.

Within ten minutes the projector was set up, and an old-fashioned portable screen on a tripod was set up, the screen extended upward.

One of the maintenance men asked, "Is there anything more, Mr. Wells?"

"That will be all, thank you," he replied, then continued to those in the room as the men left. "Kamryn needs to make a presentation which requires visuals." He held his finger to his lips, and the men all nodded in understanding. They turned to her. She was on.

Kamryn stood and smiled nervously. All eyes were on her, and their faces were stern. "Do you have an overhead marker I can use, Mr. Wells?" He got Sharon to bring one in, and after a bit, she was able to begin.

"I had a revelation, so to speak, I guess." She began to write on the projector's plastic film, taking the time she needed to ensure she left nothing of importance out. When she was finished, she flipped the light on, casting the message onto the screen. She took her seat.

After only a couple of minutes, all eyes turned back to her. Homeland Security director Miles James was the first to speak. "Are you sure about this, Kamryn?"

"Positive, Mr. James," she replied. "I just can't

proceed without the following."

She stood once again and cranked the film on the projector until it was blank. She began writing. She needed to know what they thought, what resources were at her disposal for use in blocking the signal, and they needed to have an attack plan ready. She wrote that whatever she used to block the signal, Josh would write the code to implement the process effectively. Essentially, the ball was in their court. Before turning the light back on, she made sure to let them know to be cautious of their words, if not silent. She wrote, "Careful what you say" at the bottom of the film.

After they read this message, Henry Whitaker asked Wells for paper and pen. He produced four additional tablets and four sharpened pencils for their use. The written conversation began.

Whitaker: How can you be sure this signal is the real deal?

Kamryn: Absolutely. I have been doing this a long time, and this is a completely foreign signal which is being sent from a region of space not compatible with any of the Earth's own satellites. I know these and their signals well.

Wood: What type of plan do you have in mind?

Kamryn: The ships have a number of personal weapons, a force field, and a single shot weapon capable of nuclear-type destruction. Total annihilation, I would say. If we find a way to block the signal, it will render all three of these, as well as the computers themselves, impotent.

President Mason: Do you have any ideas on how to go about this?

Kamryn: I need to know what our resources are before I can even begin to put two and two together, and it would be pointless to implement a block without an attack plan in order.

The men all looked at each other, then Miles James began writing on his own tablet. He passed it to Mason, and it made its rounds to all the men in charge. Finally, they got back to Josh and Kamryn.

President Mason: There is no way to have all this together by tomorrow morning.

Kamryn: I wouldn't think so, but if we are all the last to be herded we don't have to worry about it. With the right resources, planning, and implementation we can get this done before testing is complete and transport begins, no problem.

Woods: It's obvious we will not be able to entirely avoid the herding process, but we must do what we can to fight back and maintain our right to life and freedom against these interlopers.

Mason: We need to meet secretly and figure out the best course of action. This needs to be done with military heads, and we need to determine how we will block, or even eradicate, the Oppressors signal. Kamryn and Josh, take the next couple of hours to yourselves. Shower or do whatever you need to do. We will confer, carefully, and call you back up soon.

Whitaker: Yes. We need to begin ASAP.

With that, Josh and Kamryn rose to leave.

"Thank you, gentleman. We will talk to you soon," he stated. Taking Kamryn by the elbow, he guided her out of the office.

Once they were in the elevator, she breathed a sigh of relief. "That went better than I'd planned. I figured they would be so doubtful that they wouldn't want to listen."

"No one can risk it by not taking the chance. It sounds incomprehensible, even to me, the fact that you tracked the signal the way you did; I am so impressed, Kamryn." Josh looked over at her. She was looking at him in a way that simply captured his heart, her eyes soft, and full of love.

He moved closer to her and taking her face gently in his hands he tilted her head back, lowering his mouth to hers. Her lips were soft and tasted sweet. His tongue made its way into her mouth and found hers. Her arms went around him, and she seemed to completely melt against his body.

The elevator door opened. He pulled away from her without looking up and realizing he had an erection he used his tablet of paper to cover it. He smiled at her and took her hand. She smiled back and wrapped her fingers around his hand.

They made their way to the office, making small talk along the way. "I need to get a shower in the gym before we get back to work," he said.

"Me too. I wish I had some clean jeans to wear, but it looks like we are going to be up all night anyway, what, with the Oppressors emerging in the morning. I have sweatpants clean, so that will have to do." They entered the office, and both grabbed their clothing and, with cell phones in hand, made their way to the gym and showers.

Twenty minutes later, Kamryn was back in the office. She had grabbed the wrong t-shirt; the one she took had been too dirty to wear again, so she wore it back and was in the process of changing into her clean one. She left her bra off; it too needed washing.

Suddenly Josh entered the office. Startled, Kamryn spun around, covering herself with her t-shirt. He looked at her, and she recognized the look in his eyes. She made no effort to turn around and put the shirt on. With his eyes glued to her, Josh gently shut the office door behind him and turned the small lock on the knob.

"Kamryn…" Josh didn't know what to say, but his eyes were saying it all. She slowly lowered the shirt, baring her breasts before him. His gaze drifted downward, his eyes lighting up as they went. She dropped the shirt to the floor without even realizing she had done so.

Josh slowly walked over to her. He put one hand on the back of her neck and began to gently kiss her once again. She responded to his lips eagerly, almost as though she were starving. His right hand found her breast, and his thumb stroked her nipple in circular motions. Goosebumps broke out all over her body.

Her hands found their way under his shirt, and she caressed his back. He lowered her to the floor to find a more comfortable position for them both. They lay there kissing passionately. He stopped only to kiss her forehead, then her cheeks, her chin. He made his way down her neck, taking his time and enjoying her scent. She let out a gentle sigh of pleasure which only served to drive him on.

Soon his mouth was on her nipple, gently nibbling and licking it until it was rock hard. Her hand found its way between his legs and stroked him. He was as hard as her nipples. In seconds he could barely contain himself. He sat up on his knees and pulled his shirt over his head, not bothering with the buttons. She reached for the fly of his jeans, smiling up at him.

Within seconds they were both completely naked, and they kissed, their bodies moving together in synchronized mutual passion. Small moans escaped her lips, and her hips began to grind and arch against him. He could take it no more. In one movement he was inside her, and she let out a small cry of pleasure.

Soon they were meeting each other stroke for stroke. His hands were tangled in her long hair, his lips glued to hers. Her breathing became heavier and heavier, and suddenly her body went rigid. Her hips arched violently as she came, and she grabbed him, pulling him deeper into her.

That was all it took. The feel of her, the sounds she made, and her scent set him over the edge. He groaned loudly as he climaxed, thrusting himself into her over and over again until they were both spent. Their sweat mingled together as he collapsed on top of her.

They lay like that for a few moments before Kamryn

began to giggle. He raised his head and looked into her eyes. "What's so funny?" He asked.

"Absolutely nothing. I'm just happy. Funny that I could be so happy at a time like this, isn't it?" Kamryn smiled at him and blushed. "I only wish I could have known you before all this."

Josh smiled back. "I understand everything you just said. I'm pretty damn happy myself right now. I don't want to waste a minute of the time we have together Kam."

After a while, they separated and pulled themselves together. While they were dressing, the intercom on Josh's desk buzzed rudely.

"Josh, Kamryn, Wells here," came the voice of their boss. "I have a bit of information the two of you will be needing. Can you come up to my office pronto?"

Josh answered, "Yes sir. Be there momentarily."

R.W.K. Clark

CHAPTER 11

Once they had sat down, Wells began to fill them in.

"We are trying to move as quickly as possible, as time is of the essence. The men are putting together a strategy," then he stopped and reached for his tablet and pen. He pulled his desk chair over to the two of them and began to write. In a few moments, he handed the pad to Josh, who leaned closer to Kam so she could read it as well.

He had written: Men putting together a battle plan. Since the signal is coming from space, other side of the ship, we are sort of at a loss as to what could be used to block it, or even shut it off entirely. Our lack of ideas and thoughts is heavy and mentally confusing. Getting desperate. Any ideas?

When they were done reading, Josh looked at her. She seemed to be staring at the floor, and she showed no sign of giving an immediate response. He began to write that they would diligently look for an option, but suddenly she put her hand over his and stopped him.

"Confusing…" was all she said for a moment.

Wells spoke. "What is it, Kamryn? What is confusing you? Do you not understand what I said?"

"No, no, I understand your words completely, but I think you just gave me the solution, or at least the beginnings of it." She took the tablet and pen out of Josh's hands and, lowering her head over it, began to write feverishly.

Momentarily, she looked up. A smile was spread across her face, and she said, "I think I have it, guys." She handed the tablet back to Josh, and the two men shared it as they read.

Soon Wells looked at her. Josh soon followed, and they were both grinning.

"This sounds feasible, Kamryn, even to a layman like me," stated Wells. "This sounds like something that can be realistically done. Do you think you can pull it off?"

She nodded vigorously. "With Josh doing his thing for me, I know I can. I'm not sure how long it will take, but I can do it."

Her idea consisted of not blocking the original signal; rather, Kamryn wanted to provide a decoy signal. This new signal would scramble theirs while giving the appearance that things were business as usual for the ships and their systems. In reality, Kamryn would have complete control, or at least, the government would. The only foreseeable obstacle would be any firewall the Oppressors were using, and overcoming it would be the biggest task. Certainly, they had one, particularly since they knew the level of technology available on Earth. She planned to infiltrate their system by disguising a hostile signal as their own. They wouldn't even know what hit them, and it would enable her to keep their ships in the air while disarming their weapons and dropping their force fields. The best part was that it would require nothing as far as equipment or resources. Nothing except the skills and experience she and Josh already possessed.

Wells began, "You two get to work. I'm going to contact the boys. Better yet, I'm going to call and let them know I am coming down for a face-to-face. The three of us are going to be here for a while so I will check in with you periodically to check on the progress of the project. Sound good to you?"

They both nodded and rose from their chairs. Wells did the same, extending his hand to shake both of theirs before walking them to the door of his office and seeing them out. He shut it gently behind them.

Back in their office, they got to work right away. In writing, Kamryn told Josh what his job would be: using their current knowledge of the Oppressors' language, she would need him to write code which would assist her in visualizing the digital signal being used by their system. She needed to understand it inside and out if they were to develop a convincing and effective decoy. Until that was finished, she was powerless. It would be no good to begin the hacking process until he had the code complete, then she could assist him in the development of the new signal.

He was on it and was convinced he knew just how to go about the task she had given him. "I'll tell you what, you go get us some food and a couple of drinks and I will get started. Until this is complete, you get the honors of doing all the running." He smiled and winked at her.

"Absolutely. Any preference for the food and drink?" She kissed him lightly yet lovingly on the lips, and when she pulled away, he simply shook his head.

"I trust you," he replied. He no longer felt like they were running in place. Confusing the ships with a false signal was ingenious. He could see the light at the end of the tunnel.

She rose, squeezed his shoulder affectionately, and left the office. He turned back to his computer, grabbing a fresh tablet from his drawer. He then sharpened some pencils in his electric sharpener. A pen would not do for this job. Then Josh cracked his knuckles and shaking his head to dispel thoughts of Kamryn, he got to work.

Kamryn walked down the hall to the elevator, feeling very light on her feet indeed. Not only was she sure this was the way to deal with the Oppressors, but she was also confident they could overpower them and win this war for the lives of all humans on earth. She was also in love. Never in her life had things shone so brightly, even in the midst of the impending death and slavery which threatened them all. She felt free, and a bit giddy as well.

In the cafeteria, she chose two greasy slices of pizza, some fresh vegetables off the salad bar, a couple cups of ranch dressing for dipping, a glass of iced tea for Josh, and water for herself. She walked to the register to pay, and Helen, the regular cashier, looked up and smiled at her.

"I can't let you pay for that, Ms. Reynolds. Mr. Wells has said that any food would be on the house for you and Mr. Nichols until further notice."

Kamryn was surprised. "Thanks, Helen. He didn't say a word to us, but we certainly appreciate it." She left the cafeteria feeling that things couldn't be more perfect if the Oppressors had never arrived. She felt incredible, in fact.

Back on her floor, she entered the office. "I hope greasy pizza and veggies are okay. I needed some real food, and nothing says real like grease, broccoli, and celery sticks."

He looked up at her and smiled. "That's fine. Just set it here, and I'll get to it soon."

She put his food on his desk and sat down to eat her own. She didn't bother him, but she was tempted to put her hands on him constantly. She couldn't wait until all of this was over so they could enjoy each other properly. She wanted to get to know him without the pressures of world catastrophe looming over them like the shadow of Death himself. It was a good plan. Now they just needed to beat the clock before it was too late, and that carried a heavy pressure all its own.

Around a half-hour later, Josh took a breather to eat his now cold pizza. He seemed to inhale it, and once he was done, he grabbed the tablet they were using to communicate and began to write a message for her.

He wrote:

"I'm on a roll. This is going to be easier than I thought. I don't think these slimeballs believe we can think on this level. With the knowledge of the language that we have, I should be able to get this written with lightning speed. I may even surprise myself. You should lie down and rest if you want. I'm going to be pounding away for a time, babe."

Kamryn read the note and nodded at him. "If you need anything make sure you wake me up. Don't hesitate, Josh, okay?"

"I won't, but I don't anticipate I need much more than time. If you rest up, you will be in perfect shape to dive in with me when you wake. Before you do though you should run and grab me a stiff coffee. Would you do that for me please?"

She nodded and smiled, leaving the office. Josh would likely need as much coffee as he could get. She walked to the receptionist's desk near the elevator.

"I'm going to need a pot of stiff coffee for Josh. As black and thick as you can get it please."

The receptionist was not someone she was familiar with; she assumed the woman was from another unit and covering for an exhausted regular. "Sure thing. I'll whip one up and get it to your office right away. Will you need anything else?"

"No, but if you could bring one every couple of hours that would be great. I'm going to catch a few z's, but Josh is going to be hard at work, and we are all aware of the deadline we are facing," Kamryn replied.

The woman nodded. "No problem. The large office

at the end of the hall, correct? Should I knock each time?"

"No, not tonight, that won't be necessary. I will tell him you will be warming up the pot periodically. Thanks. We appreciate it." Kamryn then went back to the office and filled Josh in on the coffee situation. She then lay down on the couch they had brought for that purpose. She covered up with a standard Army issue green wool blanket, and even though it was afternoon, she fell asleep very quickly, her dreams just out of the grasp of her memory.

She jerked awake suddenly, her open eyes searching for Josh immediately. He sat at the computer, hard at work. His fingers tapped away at a deathly rate of speed, and in her semi-confused state, she found herself wondering if this single task would result in carpal tunnel for the code writer.

"How's it going?" She sat up on the couch, yawning and stretching.

He answered her without turning around. "Better than I could have possibly hoped. I completely understand the signal. It is really, really simple. I'm about a third of the way through the code. Won't know how it works until the test run, but I should have this done in less than a week. Just getting into the meat and potatoes of it now."

"What time is it?" She asked.

"Just after one in the morning. You slept so good you were even snoring," he stopped and spun to face her in his desk chair. "It was really cute. You must have needed it."

Just then the office door opened and the haggard-looking receptionist came in with a brown and black thermal carafe of fresh coffee. "Hello, sleepy-head," she said to Kamryn, smiling. "My turn is next. My relief will be here at two, and I get her place on the couch in the administration break room. Feel better?"

"Oh, yeah. Absolutely. A cup of that will finish the wake-up process perfectly." She smiled back at the woman and rose to pour herself a cup.

In minutes she was seated at her desk, sipping the steaming liquid and watching Josh over her shoulder. She didn't speak, for fear of interrupting his thought process, and she didn't know a thing about writing code, but it looked like he was on a roll. She closed her eyes and moved her head in a circular motion to stretch her neck muscles. She felt more rested than she had in a long time. Maybe the great sex had something to do with it?

After another half-hour and few cups of coffee later, Josh stopped typing and stretched his fingers out, popping his knuckles. He raised his arms over his head for a full-body stretch, groaning as he went. He then turned to Kamryn.

"I'm gonna bop up and down the hall a couple of times to get the blood flowing. I'll be right back, okay?" She nodded in response, and he rose and left the office.

She poured herself a third cup and then called up the receptionist's desk. After three rings she heard the tired voice. "Yes?"

"This is Kamryn. Could you please have your relief bring a fresh pot, and let her know we will need another one in an hour now that I'm awake?"

She replied, "Sure. I'm doing a shift transfer now, so she should be there within the next fifteen minutes or so. Will that do?"

"Yes. Thanks again." She replaced the receiver and sat back in her desk chair, rocking it slightly. She found the motion to be comforting, to say the least.

Soon Josh was back. He sat and faced her.

"By the time this is done, regardless of the circumstances, we should be able to develop the precise program for what we need. There may be a few bugs, initially, but I'm confident in my ability to iron them out if they are there." He yawned and poured a coffee, slugged it down, then refilled the cup. He shook the pot. "This is a dead soldier," he said and set it back on the desk.

Kamryn smiled at him. "Yes. I already spoke to Reception, and they will be bringing another shortly, then again every hour after."

"Good thinking. I should know I can count on you to be thinking. Back to work for me, Cutie." He smiled and leaned forward. She did the same, and they enjoyed a leisurely kiss before he dove back into the trenches.

Kamryn busied herself with notes regarding the false signal and the implantation of their leg of the plan. She knew that the boys upstairs were likely planning military attack, but she also knew that the Oppressors were going to be disembarking from the ships to begin the herding in six hours. The thought made her stomach lurch with fear and trepidation. What would they look like? How would they act toward the people of Earth? All of it was incomprehensible, and she could barely handle thinking about it. She put her focus back on her notes and kept it there.

An hour and two more pots of coffee later Josh stood to stretch out again. "Moving a bit slower now that I'm in the thick of it. Five hours and counting. I can barely stand the anxiety I feel when I think about seeing these damn aliens, Kam."

"I know. I feel the same way. I have been taking notes and planning just to keep my mind off of the reality of it. There really is nothing we can do but buck up. It's coming, faster than any of us would like." She stared into her coffee cup, concentrating hard on keeping the tears of fear from spilling out of her eyes.

He walked over and stood behind her chair, and placing his hands on her shoulders, began to massage. He leaned down and whispered in her ear, "Don't cry, Kam. I'm here, and I'll die before I let them separate us. They will have to kill me first."

She spun her chair so that she was facing him. "Really? You would do that, Josh? Aren't you afraid?" The tears won, and they danced down both cheeks. Her eyes were so beautiful, as though the tears enhanced them. It took his breath away.

"In a heartbeat. Without a second thought."

She put down her cup and stood, wrapping her arms around him, seeking the shelter of his embrace. He hugged her tightly to him and inhaled her scent. Soon she raised her chin, and looking into his eyes, she kissed him. It didn't take long before the feel of her began to get the best of him, and it took everything inside of him to break their kiss.

"We can't babe. We don't have time. You know I want to, but we don't have time." His voice was as gentle and soothing as it could be.

"Can't we just die making love and say screw the world? At least then I would die in your arms." Her tears were falling freely now. She was scared to death, but so was he.

He spoke, "We have to stay focused. The fact is, the world needs us. It's apparent we were put here for this time, Kamryn. We are responsible because of our knowledge, and even though we didn't ask for it, we set ourselves up for sure."

She simply nodded and sat back down. He moved over to his own chair and did the same, winking at her before turning back to his computer screen and keyboard. Time to get back to it.

Eight o'clock was just around the corner if the Oppressors didn't emerge sooner.

R.W.K. Clark

CHAPTER 12

Sunrise came threateningly.

At seven, Josh stopped working and began to pace the office. She did the same. At seven-fifteen, the intercom buzzed, and Wells' voice echoed from it.

"How are the two of you doing?"

Josh answered, "Work-wise things are going very, very well. Emotionally, I'd say we are both a bit frazzled."

"Well, if this helps, word came from the White House at six that we are not required to rally in the streets to greet them. We can stay in our homes or places of work. The armed forces, all branches, with the President and his men, will be the ones to greet the Oppressors. We are going to be taking this a step at a time. The other ships will not begin to come out until the Commander in Chief has met with the leader and spokesperson of and for the Oppressors." His voice sounded somber, and just as afraid as they felt.

Josh and Kamryn both breathed a major sigh of relief. He replied, "So we can continue to work and remain in the office until further notice?"

"Yes," replied Wells. "We know they are going to let

government people on all levels get herded for testing last. You will know as soon as I do. Keep up the good work, you two. Don't let emotions get the best of you. I'll be in touch."

The speaker on the intercom went dead, and both Josh and Kamryn released a rush of breath that was audible.

"What a relief. I can't even tell you, but I'm sure you know anyway," Josh said.

Kamryn answered with a shaky voice. "I don't think there are words to describe the relief."

"I'm going to get back to work. The sooner we get this done, the sooner the real games begin." Josh leaned forward and kissed her, the love he felt tangible in his kiss. He pulled away and said, "Soon you will be able to start giving them what they deserve."

He turned to his computer, and Kamryn excused herself to go to the restroom. Once she was in the stall with the door firmly locked, she lost control and began to weep uncontrollably. For the next ten minutes, her thin frame was racked with sobs. Finally, she emerged from the stall and washed her face at one of the sinks along the wall. She dried her face with a paper towel and made sure the redness in her eyes had subsided before joining Josh back in their office.

∞

President Andrew Mason and his men sat in the back of a sleek black limousine parked at the Washington Monument, the designated meeting place for himself, his men, the leader of the Oppressors, and the leader's crew. His stomach roiled violently with fear, and it was terribly difficult to hide the tremor in his hands. Miles James and Carson Wood sat with him, but none of them spoke. They all had a snifter of brandy to calm their nerves. It was vital that they show no weakness to the enemy. They needed to be calm and confident, displaying only strength. He wasn't sure if he could do it. They didn't even know what these beings looked like. The mere sight of them could incite hysteria, for all he knew.

At 7:50, he looked at the other men.

"It's time."

They put down their snifters almost simultaneously and got out of the back of the limo. All branches of the armed forces were already there and in place. They were the last to arrive.

In between the monument and the Lincoln Memorial Reflecting Pool was where the meet would take place in only moments. Flanked by his men, and surrounded by secret service, President Mason took his place, and as they all stood there, they stared upwards at the ship's underbelly, waiting for some sign of a door opening. None of them had any idea what to expect, not only from the ship but from the Oppressors as well.

At precisely 8:00 A.M. Eastern Standard Time the hatch began to open.

The ship was vast and black, with lights scattered across its surface, but almost directly over the place where the president and the other men were situated, and in the midst of some of the lights, the ship's surface seemed to almost dissolve. The material the ship was made of began to waterfall toward the earth below, touching down immediately in front of the President, the Secretary of Defense, and the Director of Homeland Security. It then solidified before their very eyes, forming what resembled a playground slide the color of slate, and the surface appeared to move.

President Mason realized he wasn't breathing, and forced himself to slowly inhale and exhale. He couldn't afford to hyperventilate and pass out, though that was the preferred course of action at the moment. This was the thing nightmares were made of.

Suddenly, at the opening of the ship, three figures appeared, and they began to come down toward the ground. It appeared they were walking, but as they got closer, it became apparent that they weren't walking. The ramp they were on was in motion like a moving walkway in an airport terminal.

The Oppressors did not appear to be much different than humans. Once their feet touched terra firma, it was obvious they were taller than the average Earthling by about a foot. Their physical structure was similar, with the main differences being their hands, their eyes, and their hairlines, which were receded quite drastically on top while their hair was worn long, almost flowing over their shoulders. They appeared to have the same colors of hair as any human being.

The three Oppressors who stood before the President and his men had dark skin; a deep, rich brown pigment. Their hands consisted of only three fingers and one thumb. Their eyes bore the most disturbing difference of all: while they had colored irises, the pupils were elongated, like those of reptiles. Their clothing appeared to be a standard military type, gray and black in color. The only way to differentiate between the outfits was by the variety of medals which the different Oppressors wore. It could be safely assumed that these items told which being held which rank in their 'army.' All three were very muscular and coupled with their taller height, this feature gave them an appearance which made them look much larger than humans in general. This, too, was a bit disturbing to the human men who stood before them, as did the unknown weapons at their thighs.

"President Mason," said the Oppressor in the middle. "My name is unpronounceable to you. I will accept you referring to me as Superior. I am the leader of my peoples."

President Mason cleared his throat and focused on keeping his voice steady and even. "As you know, I am President Andrew Mason. I am the leader of this country on planet Earth." He gestured to each of the men by his side. "This is Miles James, Director of Homeland Security for the United States of America, and this is Carson Wood, Secretary of Defense." He turned and cast his eyes over the vast groups of military men and women who stood at attention behind him. "These individuals make up our military teams in the United States."

Superior nodded, taking it all in. He looked back at Mason. "To my right is Secondary, and to my left is Subordinate. We will discuss the facilities, the testing of your people, our expectations, and your outcome. Will we talk here? We would rather sit as to not intimidate."

Mason was at a bit of a loss. The last thing he wanted to do was separate himself and his men from the military forces who stood waiting to protect them. He looked to his right and his left, making eye contact with the men who accompanied him, completely unsure of the wisest course of action.

"Since we are all strangers, I believe our meeting should take place in the open. To be honest, we do not feel a rapport with you. From our standpoint, your visit is completely hostile. You are here to take our freedoms and eliminate us from our own home planet, by your own admission." He turned to Miles James. "Call and have someone bring a long folding table and the appropriate number of folding chairs right away." Miles immediately got on his cellular phone and carried out the president's order.

Mason continued. "In the meantime, we can begin if you would like."

A slight smile played at Superior's narrow mouth. "Very well. The testing facilities all over this planet have made wonderful progress in their construction. These facilities are vital to the process of determining who shall continue their lives and who will lose them by elimination. We are pleased that your people have been so expeditious in carrying out our commands, and because we are pleased, we have granted certain peoples here leniency, such as your governing workers.

"Know that while you refer to us as hostile, you should also credit us with what we deserve. The strongest and most intelligent of yours will be granted survival. This will enable you to continue your lives at a distant place which has been prepared for you. We are aware that you have questioned whether we were making the determination for the weak or the strong. It is sincerely not our intention to completely eliminate your race. We will give you the opportunity to start over. The only people you will lack are those who will serve only to slow down the process."

Now it was Secondary's turn to speak. This being's voice was even deeper than the first's. "The testing will have a number of aspects that you should be aware of as the leader of your peoples. It will be you who will control the level of panic and chaos which will inevitably take place as the herding begins today. Know that families will be separated for the sake of efficiency. Know that many will not see each other ever again. Most in fact. This is the herding process."

Right then three human men approached from the rear. They carried a long, conference-type folding table and gray metal folding chairs. Mason and his crew stepped back a few feet to allow for the setting up of these items, as did Superior and his men. Within moments they were seated, and the conversation resumed.

"We must have sun," Superior began.

Mason waited expectantly for him, or one of them, to elaborate. Finally, he broke the silence. "What does this have to do with taking our planet and killing our people?"

Subordinate explained, "We are far too many to cohabitate with you; you are all wasting your own resources at an alarming rate. A period of two Earth-months ago, our sun disappeared from our skies. The end result was the death of the planet we call home." He paused and looked upward, and seeing only his own ship, he looked back at Mason and continued. "Your planet has what our people need. It is simple. Our people can continue to thrive here."

"Why not just make a new one for yourselves? The same way you are supposedly making one for us? Nothing you are saying makes any sense, and this is why we doubt your word." Mason's voice was a bit stern in his delivery.

Suddenly, Superior slammed his fist down on the meager folding table, making it shake violently, and he raised his deep, gravelly voice to a fever pitch.

"We are merciful! We did not opt to simply destroy you all, as we well could have, and perhaps should have, done! There will be no questioning! You will simply comply."

The President's hands, woven together atop the table before him, began to tremble slightly, and his stomach lurched at the thunderous sound of anger in Superior's voice. "So tell us your plan, Superior."

"The people will be herded from each area

incrementally, and they will be taken to the facilities determined by us as we see fit. This will begin as soon as this meeting is over." The word meeting dripped with sarcasm as it came out of his mouth. "Tests will consist of physical strength determination, intelligence, physical health, including testing of your biological make-up. These will help determine the strongest and most viable humans for transfer. You will all also be tested to determine the most creative and educated. You will need physicians and individuals who can design and build if you want to grow and thrive in your new home. Those who are transferred will need to be skilled in hand to hand combat; there are native creatures on the planet of your future, and you will need to defend yourselves and your new families against them. You will be given no automatic weapons of any kind."

President Mason began to feel strong nausea as the reality of the situation set in. "With whom will you begin?"

"Those living on the streets. The homeless, the addicted, and those who we deem weaker than the rest. Next will be the common man, the everyday human drone, or worker, as you may call them," stated Secondary firmly. "Your government and authorities will be very last. Those who are prosperous and living well obviously have a strength of some type. They will be herded toward the end. Believe that we have an established process. Our peoples have had to go through this for countless Earth-years."

Mason shook his head in disbelief. He wanted to

pinch himself so he would wake up from this nightmare. He wanted to jump from the roof of the White House, swan-dive, just to make sure he didn't live. He needed to pull himself together and clear his head.

"How will survivors be transported after they have been determined?" He asked.

Subordinate replied, "We have a fleet of ships to transport them in. The trip will take nearly one Earth-year. Each ship will have everything needed to sustain life for those who will be living on board for that period."

Silence fell over all of them. The three Oppressors kept their eyes on the Earthlings before them. Superior shifted in his seat. He was anxious to get started. They had waited patiently enough for too long, in his opinion.

"We will call our forces down and prepare for the process. It is time for you to address your people and give instructions. They are to return to their homes, all of them. We will check places of business and successfully clear them, but in consideration of the time, you need to keep them calm. Represent us properly. Do not make us out to be heartless monsters. If we were, you would have never seen this coming, Mason."

The President pondered this and finally nodded. "I will have a televised press conference to address my fellow citizens." With that he stood, followed by the other individuals. Mason simply nodded and turned, walking away.

CHAPTER 13

Josh rubbed his eyes and went back to diligently tapping on his keyboard. Kamryn had paced back and forth since five minutes to eight, at which time she had left the office. She returned at eight-fifteen pushing a television on a cart. She plugged it in, hooked up an old-fashioned digital adaptor box, and turned it on, keeping the volume on silent. An old re-run of 'Three's Company' danced across the screen, followed by another.

Just after nine, a newscaster appeared on the screen.

"Josh, it's time, I think." She jumped up and turned the volume on the set up as Josh turned his desk chair to watch.

"In only moments, President Mason will address the nation regarding his conference with the Oppressors. He will fill us in on what all of us can expect in the future." The screen went to the traditional podium, which was flanked by flags. Microphones with a variety of news channel logos were perched atop the podium. The television was silent, with the exception of a few scattered whispers which could be heard from the reporters who were there in person.

Andrew Mason appeared.

"My fellow Americans. Today, I have met with the Oppressors face to face. We have been told what their plans are concerning our country, our world, our existence, and our future. Before I begin, I want you to be aware that we have hope. The key to ensuring any future is full cooperation on our part. This will be vital to our existence.

"We will all be tested. They have established another planet, which will be our new home. Testing facilities and the tests they give will determine who will be granted relocation privileges. Survivors will be determined by these tests. Do the very best you can on all aspects.

"As I have stated: The Oppressors are firm in the process and the implementation of it. They will be the sole future inhabitants of Earth, but they have graciously made way for a specified number of individuals from our population to survive. Do the very best you can to be in that number.

"Do not panic. Directly after this broadcast, they will begin herding, beginning with those found on the streets and in homeless shelters, to the testing facilities. To put up a fight is to sign your own death warrant immediately, eliminating any chance for your own survival. They will conduct the herding in a chain of sorts: next will be smaller, less fortunate residential districts, and they will work their way up. Anyone employed in any manner by any level of government will be last. Continue to do your jobs diligently, as this is the only reason you are going last; your positions, authoritative and otherwise, are needed by them to expedite the herding process.

"Once more, do not fight. Cooperation is essential at this time.

"I will be taking no questions. Thank you, and God bless America and the rest of planet Earth."

Those who were listening to him in person went into an uproar. Chaos broke out in the room where President Mason and his men stood. The last thing Josh and Kamryn saw before she shut the set off was the President being rushed from the conference by Secret Service.

The two sat in silence. Neither was surprised by his words; they were essentially what they were already aware of. After a period of thought, Kamryn looked at Josh and spoke.

"I don't know how long an individual battery of tests lasts, but we need to really get busy, Josh. We don't have a moment to spare."

He replied, "You're right. Let's get to it."

∞

President Andrew Mason sat hard in his desk chair in the Oval Office. He wove his fingers together on the desk before him and stared at the picture of his wife, Sharon, and their teenage children. He wanted to see them. He wanted to hold them and tell them how much he loved them because he was unsure of anything.

Wood, James, and Whitaker sat in what had become

their regular chairs on the other side of his desk. No one knew what to say, and they were afraid to speak. Finally, Miles James broke the silence.

"Now what?"

It was amazing that such educated and highly-trained men could be so utterly lost and confused, but this event was unprecedented. It had caught them all off guard. To put it simply, there were no words.

"We are going to depend on those two kids down at the Pentagon, and we are going to hope for the best," Mason finally stated. "For now, we will go home and comfort our families as best we can."

∞

Superior stood regally before his armies, all of whom had been summoned to the Lincoln Reflecting Pool area. They stood at rapt attention by the hundreds, not one flinching or shifting in any way. They were a highly-disciplined group indeed. He began to pace back and forth in silence before them.

Secondary stood behind him and off to the side. The only thing moving on him were his snake-like eyes as he watched their leader intimidate their army with his very presence. Superior had come into his role upon the death of his father, back home on planet Kwan, more than ten Earth years ago. His name had been Senior, and he had been a good ruler. Never during his reign had the people been required to conduct planetary extermination, although they were common in the history of the Kwanite people. By nature, the Kwanites used more than they should when it came to needed resources, as did all conscious species, or so it seemed. Regardless of this fact, Senior had enacted a variety of methods which maintained the planet's resources wonderfully, and the peoples had lived a happy existence for more than fifty Earth years.

When Senior had taken ill, Superior had come into power, and he was nothing like the ruler his father was. His heart was black, and he hungered for power. Secondary was much older than Superior, though age did not show on the Kwanite people as it did on Earthlings. The fact was, Secondary had been the right-hand man of Senior for the last five Earth years of his reign. He had dreaded seeing Superior come to power. He knew how the man enjoyed harming others, and how much he enjoyed seeing even the smallest bit of fear in their eyes.

It was the mark of a true tyrant.

But come to power Superior did, here they stood on a foreign planet, overtaking it with force and instilling dread and fear into the hearts and minds of its people. His father would roll over in his universal burial capsule if he knew. The horrid part was Superior would enjoy his father knowing.

Superior stopped his pacing and faced the masses before him. He began to speak with a stern voice full of terrible purpose. "We will begin herding today." He paused for effect, looking his men over to see their reactions before continuing. "You are all quite blessed and fortunate to receive your orders directly from me!"

He rose his arms in the air, pride beaming from his face, in a gesture which demanded that he be glorified.

"HEAR, HEAR SUPERIOR!" They all shouted in unison in their native tongue. This did not appease the ruler, though. He jerked his arms upward more violently, a sneer now on his face.

Louder now, "HEAR, HEAR SUPERIOR!!"

This seemed to placate the evil in the leader's heart, and he put his arms down and continued. "Proceed, Kwanite Army!"

The footmen raised both arms in the air, pointing all fingers together toward the sky in salute. They then began to disperse in a very orderly and uniform manner.

∞

The Oppressors' main military leader for that sector stood before his men, who were lined up uniformly in the middle of Pennsylvania Avenue and were facing toward the more shoddy area of town. They would begin marching, herding as they went. They had very specific methods of determining who would be part of the first group of test participants. They would be the transients, anyone found loitering or living outdoors. They were told these individuals would be dirty, with filthy clothing and far-away eyes. The hair upon their heads would be unclean, as well. They would have no purpose.

'Leader' was the general for this sector's military. He stood before his men, who filled the street for eight full blocks, and his eyes scanned a computerized clipboard-type device he held in his hands. He took in the information, scanned it again, and then looked up at his men.

"The first battalion will take the first assigned quadrant in the initial radius. The second, the third, and so on. Men, let the herding begin!" He beat the air with a clenched right fist, and his men all followed suit, a battle-cry emitting from their lips.

Initially, they marched, but each battalion soon separated from the others. The first to be taken was a man with scraggly hair sleeping on a bus stop bench. The second was a prostitute, barely dressed, who was hiding between two small storefronts trying to get one final fix. Each battalion would herd until each member had one individual. They would then take the people to a wheeled ground transport vehicle, which would take them to their assigned facility to begin testing.

The first day was the easiest the people of Earth would see in regard to the herding. The people gathered had no families to speak of; they were the dregs of society, the losers, the unloved and unwanted. The vast number of military Oppressors made the herding of these individuals easy. It wasn't until it was time to go into the rundown residences in search of the poor and lowly that things would begin to get very serious indeed.

∞

Kamryn picked at a green salad. She had no real appetite. Why eat? She had left Josh to continue writing the golden code she so desperately needed, partly because she didn't want to distract him, but mostly because if she had to listen to those keys tapping for another second, she would go off the deep end.

She picked up her iced tea and drained the glass, thinking about the latest news updates. A chill ran through her body. The herding had ceased as the facilities became full with the first batch of test subjects: the homeless and addicted. Oppressors lined the streets, waiting for the initial tests to end, and maintaining order. Mostly, they were observing, learning, and planning. It reminded Kamryn of a cat watching a mouse.

The first battery of tests had ended after one week, and the herding began again. This time they were herding people from the worst part of town. They dragged them from the apartments. Some went willingly, others kicking and screaming. Children were taken forcefully from their welfare-recipient parents, and the news showed the dirty tear-streaked faces of toddlers and young children as they held out their arms to their parents, sobbing and crying.

That herding process lasted a day and a half. Television cameras picked up video of the herding, and their faces bore humorless smiles which seemed to go entirely against all that was taking place.

The press had been directed to limit the reports given to the public due to the fact that the Oppressors were all eyes and ears. The video was the only thing that gave the people an idea of what to expect, and it was horrifying for all to see.

Kamryn took her tray with all of her salad, virtually

untouched, and tossed it in the waste receptacle nearest the door. She threw away the paper cup which had held her now-drained iced tea, and she left the cafeteria. The elevator ride seemed to take forever, and the silence within only emphasized her feeling of helpless suffocation. She needed a release.

She entered the office and locked the door behind her. Coming up behind Josh, she began to gently massage his shoulders. He moaned, his typing halting momentarily.

"Hi. Did you eat?" He asked.

"Not really." She let her hands creep down to his chest, massaging their way. He finally stopped typing and allowed himself to enjoy her touch. She bent down and kissed his neck, following that gesture by running her tongue down his nape. She continued with tiny licks and light kisses until he gave in and turned in his chair.

"I need this, Josh. Don't say no. We have time." He didn't say no. Instead, he stood to his feet and began to undo the buttons on the blouse she was wearing. She reciprocated. Soon, both of their shirts lay on the floor behind them. She planted her lips firmly on his, invading his mouth with her tongue almost violently. She pressed herself forcefully against him and grabbed handfuls of his curly, dark hair. He kissed her back hard.

Finally, she pulled away from him, unbuttoned her jeans, and dropped them to the floor as well. He simply watched her, a small smile on his face. She removed her bra and tossed it like the annoyance that it was. She then dropped to her knees before him and began to work on the button on his jeans. Within seconds, she took him in her mouth, and a long groan escaped his lips.

"Damn, Kamryn. Wow." He was growling deep in his throat.

She worked him into a frenzy, and soon he had to pull himself away from her before he lost his resolve. He pulled her to her feet and sat her on the couch.

"Don't lie down; just sit there."

She did, and soon he was on his knees before her, returning the favor. Her eyes were closed in ecstasy, her mouth wide open. Her fingers tangled themselves in his hair. All she was aware of was his lips and tongue, and she ground herself against his face. Suddenly her hips arched violently, and she rocked back and forth against his mouth in her orgasm.

He mounted her forcefully, and soon they writhed together like animals, sweating and groaning. She came again, along with him, and finally, they both lay on the couch, spent and smiling.

After about fifteen minutes, Josh spoke. "I am going to be done with the code and begin testing with a false signal by the end of the week, Kam."

She opened her eyes and looked at him. "Really, Josh?"

"Really."

She sat up. Yes! Once they did the testing and got any needed troubleshooting out of the way, they could get the interfering signal sent!

"Let's shower so you can get back to work. I'm not going to keep you." She hopped up and gathering her clothes, began to quickly dress. He did the same while she grabbed her hygiene items. "I'll see you back here in a few minutes?"

He smiled and nodded at her as she left the room. He was right behind her.

∞

Peter Wells sat in his office watching the latest news broadcast on the herding. Many of the cities were further along than Washington in the process, but some of them didn't have the homeless and addicted population Washington did. The media didn't expand much with information: the video spoke for itself. The only thing they did state was that the second group of test subjects would be done in one week as well. Obviously, the testing was designed to last only seven days. The third group, low-income families with blue-collar workers, would be next.

He picked up the remote control and shut off the set. He was so tired of watching, but it was the only way to monitor the progress. He couldn't just ignore what was happening. For the sake of his own loved ones, he had to keep current.

He had spoken to Josh and Kamryn the evening before, and Josh made him aware he would be done with the current phase of their plan within the week. Sure, it had only been last night, but maybe he was further than he thought he would be. He reached for the intercom and pushed the button.

"Sharon, please have Josh call me on my office

phone," he requested.

"Yes, sir," she replied.

In less than thirty seconds, his phone chirped, and he picked it up anxiously. "How is it going today, Josh?"

"Very well, sir. Still anticipated the same time frame, but I'm hoping the extra work will mean fewer bugs to iron out of the end result. With luck, Kamryn will be able to put this to use by next week."

Wells replied, "Yes. I was hoping things had perhaps gone a little better today, making for a better-predicted outcome."

"It's a process, sir."

He thanked Josh and disconnected. Rising from his chair, he walked to his window and looked outside. He wished he had a better view.

He thought about his wife, kids, and grandkids. He couldn't let despair and depression take over now. They were too close. There was too much to lose by giving up.

CHAPTER 14

The second group of test subjects completed their testing, and the next herding phase was well underway. The topic of greatest concern on both the news and among those still awaiting herding had to do with those who had completed testing. No one had any idea who was passing or failing. For all they knew, people were being taken into the facilities and finding themselves the victims of mass murder. The streets were filled with emotionally charged people, particularly when the thought that humans were marching willingly, to their own deaths. Many thought simply being killed during the actual herding process made much more sense.

As those who were members of blue-collar households were gathered, it became distinctly obvious that gathering the third group was going to take a bit more time. There were far more people in this class than the previous two, at least in the civilized parts of the world. Things began to take a bit longer for the Oppressors, and it was becoming apparent that their patience was wearing thin as far as the humans were concerned. Rather than fight those who struggled, they began to murder them immediately. It was also speculated that many more humans were passing the tests than the Oppressors had anticipated.

Josh had completed writing the code for the infiltration signal right when he thought he would. Peter Wells, the President, and the President's men all gathered and determined a proper testing method. They would use it to interfere with their own Internet and satellite services, but they would do it on a limited basis to fly under the aliens' radar.

Initial tests proved a bit messy. Nothing went as planned. If humans could not interfere with their own signal successfully, how did they expect to fly an effective dummy signal to the alien ships stationed around the world? Troubleshooting and rectifying the issues would be one of the most vital aspects of the entire project, and Josh and Kam found themselves headed back to the drawing board on the first day.

But this did not prove to deter anyone. They had come too far to give up now. The entirety of Project Native had become more of a do-or-die prospect than ever before. Testing the false signal was what the hacking portion of the job was all about, so it was in Kam's hands, but without a properly developed code, her hands were tied. So, Josh reset his focus, which he expected to need to do, and went about swatting the troublesome bugs which were buzzing around their heads.

The world was into week three of the herding phase of the Oppressors' takeover efforts, and the behavior of Earth's people became more panicked and erratic than ever before.

The news reported the suicide count around the world to number in the hundreds of thousands. Bodies were being collected by local authorities all over, and no proper services were held for anyone. The Oppressors had designated body drop sites, and collectors were made to deliver bodies there regularly, where they were piled up until they reached a specific number. They were then mass-buried on the earth just as they had been found.

Out of sight, out of mind seemed to be the outlook of the invaders trolling the planet.

Smaller towns were virtually cleaned out after the third herding phase, and citizens waited on pins and needles for the third week of testing to be completed. In the meantime, the Oppressors simply scouted and re-scouted the cities and surrounding areas to which they had been assigned, tracking down anyone who belonged in the first three groups but had managed to escape capture. According to the news, these individuals were held at the facilities, crowded together, waiting for all testing to be complete so they could be dealt with.

It seemed that the Oppressors had overlooked one particular group of individuals, and this group consisted of many, many people. Convicts and criminals holed up in jails and penitentiaries all over the world were somehow unrecognized by the aliens. Once aware of their existence, Superior had sent extra forces into these places, and their testing took place right where they were. This eliminated the hassle, and danger, which transporting the outcasts would potentially bring. Just as in life before the Oppressors, the outcome of these forgotten lives remained unknown.

The fourth day into the week of Phase 3, Josh announced that the code could be re-tested, and once again the powers that be accompanied him and Kamryn for the tests. The second bug they encountered proved to be small compared to the first. The signal was implemented, but it kept crashing.

Back to work for Josh.

By day six, they were able to try it yet again, and while it worked on close range satellites, it proved to fail when it came to reaching as far as they needed it to go.

This was a worldwide project after all. More work.

Day seven of Phase 3 came and went, and groups of middle-to-upper class families were herded and hauled in for testing. Herding these people was set to take place over three weeks to ensure the capture of everyone in the group. Dead bodies, both from suicides and Oppressor elimination continued to pile up, and the aliens continued to seek out anyone who had successfully escaped.

On day two of Phase 4, Josh and Kamryn sat in their office, which had become a prison cell to them now. They cherished the testing times because they got to breathe outside air, even though they never saw the light of the sun.

Josh was tapping away at his keyboard like any other time, but his patience was wearing thin. He would burst out in profanities every now and then, and even though the office was air-conditioned, he seemed to have a perpetual film of sweat on his upper lip. Kamryn, too, was nearly at the end of her rope. She found herself pacing, even losing patience with Josh on more than one occasion. Today was one of those times.

Kam had been at the cafeteria drinking sludge-black coffee. She had made small talk with a few of the other employees and even attempted to engage herself in a game of cribbage with a co-worker. Halfway through the game, she felt as though she might crawl out of her skin. It just wasn't right that she was playing a card game at a time like this, even if it was just to pass the time until she could fully implement her strategy. She apologized to the woman she was playing with, saying only. "I just can't do this. I'm sorry." She had risen from her seat and left the cafeteria in a huff.

Now she was walking back to the elevator. What was Josh doing, anyway? Did she seriously need to light a fire under his ass? She thought he would be finished with his part of the job way before now, and it was beginning to feel like they were going to be herded, tested, and gotten rid of without ever putting her plan into action.

It was a good plan! No, it was better than good; it was great. Not to mention it was the only way. He needed to get on the stick. She jabbed at the elevator button impatiently, over and over, until she heard the 'Ding!' Announcing its arrival. As she stepped onto the elevator, she realized her forefinger was bleeding. She had broken a nail pushing that damn button. Furious, she lit from the conveyance and puffed her way to their office. He had better not be sleeping. Maybe he needed more help getting this job done than he had been willing to admit. It was time to have a serious talk with Josh.

She opened the office door and tore right in, slamming and locking it behind her.

"Josh, we seriously need to discuss what the heck is taking so long with this project!" She grabbed the back of his desk chair and spun it around.

His eyes were red-rimmed and wide. He was obviously mad that she had so rudely interrupted his work, but his voice gave away nothing. "What's wrong with you, Kam?"

She plopped into her own chair. "What's wrong with me? I'll tell you what's wrong with me!" She pointed her broken, bleeding finger at him and continued. "We are in week four of testing and herding, and while you have gotten rid of some of the bugs, we are only running in place! If you need extra help, why don't you just say so?! I know what my job is, and I can do it. So, why can't you? I mean really, dude, you have a college education, and I barely graduated high school!" Her face was red and flushed, and Josh could see she was obviously very pissed off. This fact only served to irritate him.

"Do you have any idea how hard I am working? I drink so much coffee that I have a perpetual stomach ache, I haven't showered in three days, and I honestly can't remember the last time I slept more than three hours! What is the matter with you? You'd better grow up and do it fast!"

Right then it occurred to Kamryn just how she sounded and how she was acting. Her breathing was ragged as this passed through her mind, and suddenly she broke. She put her face into her hands, spun in her chair, and sobbed. She didn't want him to see her cry after acting like such an ass to him.

In seconds, his hand was on her back as he attempted to comfort her. "Shhh. It's okay. I know how you are feeling. Just cry it out."

She kept her face turned from him, but she let him take her into his arms, and she buried herself in the solace of his embrace. Her body was wracked with sobs, and his white button-down shirt was getting soaked from her tears. He felt so hopeless and powerless. All he could do was hold her in her time of need. The world had to have her firing on all her pistons. She couldn't have a meltdown now. He was all she had. It was vital that he were there when she needed him.

After a few minutes, Kamryn pulled away from him. She reached for a box of tissue on her desk, wiped her eyes, and blew her nose. It took another three or four minutes for her to completely stop crying, but finally, her eyes met his. She looked a mess.

"I'm sorry, Josh." He said nothing back, he only shook his head in a gesture of no apology needed.

She rose and began to pace the office. She had perfected this skill.

"Kamryn, we are all under a massive amount of pressure. We can all tell time, and we all know the clock is ticking, but we have to focus on what we have instead of what is going. Phase 4 is going to be a three-week phase, minimum, and the Oppressors are so busy trying to find the ones that got away that we are the last thing on their minds. They have extra men at the prisons and jails. These are positives. Keep your eyes on these things."

She nodded at him and once again apologized. "Go back to work, Josh. I'm going to the gym to work off my fear and frustration."

He replied, "That's a great idea. I'll see you when you get back, okay Kam?" With that, he turned back to his desk, scanned the screen with his eyes, and began typing again.

She watched him only for a moment before grabbing a clean change of clothes and her hygiene items. She might as well shower when she was done working out. She was going to be down there anyway.

"Do you want me to bring food back for you?" She asked this timidly, not wanting to interrupt him even further.

He didn't even speak. He just kept tapping away and shook his head 'no.'

She left the office grieving over how she had treated him. Not only had she blown up, but she had insulted his intelligence and capabilities as well. He didn't deserve any of what he had just endured.

She arrived at the gym, put her things in an unsecured locker, and hit the weights with a vengeance. It was time to get her focus back.

CHAPTER 15

After her final set of reps on the last weight machine, Kamryn let go of the weight and relaxed on her back on the bench. She wiped sweat from her chest and face, then dropped the towel on the floor next to her and closed her eyes.

Suddenly, she was in her small one-room apartment. She was sitting at her computer working diligently. She knew what she was doing. She was hacking into the Ameribank security system in an attempt to confuse it and plant fake video footage. This would enable the 'client' who had hired her to break into the bank without giving the police any kind of alarm, and it would block his activities for a full eight hours. He would get away with millions.

She worked away, getting closer and closer to her goal. She knew exactly what steps to take, and each step was taken as smoothly and successfully as the one before it. Before she knew it, she was calling her guy.

Now she was talking to him in her room. She was telling him that she would control the bank system remotely while he pulled the job. Her stomach fluttered with excitement and eagerness. This job promised a large payout. She could get a new place to live, maybe even a car…

Kamryn suddenly jerked awake. She sat up quickly, and leaving her belongings in the locker forgotten, she ran from the gym. She needed to get to the office and talk to Josh. What about video feed? She hadn't even thought of this aspect of the Oppressors' system, and she knew they had one. That was how they were keeping such close tabs on the street people. It was how they had discovered the prisons.

She got off the elevator and ran down the hall to the office. All she could think was how desperately they needed satellite footage of Washington and all the other cities. It had to be fed into the ships' systems while they set up the attack. Without this, the Oppressors would be laughing their heads off watching the silly humans set up their strategy. Heck, they were liable to simply blow the whole place to smithereens.

She flung the office door open. "Josh, listen! I just thought of a vital point I had not even considered. I have a lot of work to do!"

Josh jumped in his seat and spun around. "Damn, Kamryn. Wow. You scared the crap out of me. What are you talking about?"

"Video! We know they have it. It runs off the same alien system we are attempting to infiltrate. I have to get satellite images of the victim cities to feed into the ships during our set up and attack, or they are going to have front row seats to our entire plan!" She sat hard on the couch, breathing heavily and sweating. "We have to talk to Wells right away!"

Josh's eyes had grown as wide as the saucers hovering in the sky. "Oh, man. I get you. I'll call him now."

Josh picked up his phone and dialed Wells' extension. "Mr. Wells. This is Josh. We need to meet with you right away." He stated a few words of agreement and hung up the phone. Grabbing his tablet and pen, he said, "Let's go, and take your paper. You may have said enough already. Let's hope they're busy."

"Maybe the video is all they ever had. They would have to have super hearing to know our plans, and if that were the case, they would be at the Pentagon already. The more I think about it, the more I believe they are dependent on video more than we think. They are monitoring us with some sort of cameras, but I'll take paper anyway."

She grabbed hers and followed him out of the office. In only minutes, they were seated in Wells' office, and Kamryn began to explain what their issue, and the resulting need, was.

"First, Mr. Wells, I want to emphasize that I do not think they can hear us, or even read our minds. I think they have been monitoring us via some sort of video recording system." At this point, she began to write on the tablet. Wells looked a bit panic-stricken at all the words flying out of her mouth. She jotted down in layman shorthand about video feed, and what she would need to successfully hack into their ships' system and plant false images to keep them sidetracked.

He read her writings, then looking up at her he asked, "Even if we feed the images, won't the guys on the ground be able to see what we are doing strategy-wise down here and attempt to fight us?"

"That's why we feed the images first, way ahead of time, as well as the fake signal. That will halt any ability they have to contact the Oppressors stationed down here, and if they try to rear their ugly heads, we can wipe them out. From what the President said, they are as mortal as we are. We just need to get a leg up. Without satellite images being fed to the ships, they will be onto us from the start."

Wells didn't hesitate. He picked up his phone and was soon online with Matthew Johnson. The next thing they knew Johnson was in Wells' office with them, and he was using Wells' phone and Kamryn's notes to communicate what was needed from the defense department and Homeland Security.

Once Johnson hung up the phone, he turned to Kamryn. "I am so relieved that you thought of this before it was too late. They are going to get us satellite footage, to be used by you as needed, of each affected area, day and night footage. Can you work things out timing wise?"

"Absolutely, but I need to set things up on my end while Josh is mending the code. Both need to be completed and implemented together, or our uprising is going to be a waste of all of our time."

Johnson nodded. "I think all of us have a very firm grasp on what you are in need of, and why you must get to work. We will plan on you having things ready to go by the time the code is in working order." He paused and looked at Kamryn thoughtfully. "I can't believe you were the true mastermind behind the Ameribank robbery. We never did catch that guy, though we knew who it was."

"I wish you would have caught him. He stiffed me on my percentage." She had anger in her eyes when she said it. "But if he would have been square with me, I wouldn't have been here to help with this. I'd have been in the Virgin Islands on the beach somewhere." She smiled grimly. Everything happens for a reason.

With that, the four parted ways, Wells and Johnson remaining in the office while Kam and Josh went back to theirs.

She had caught the mistake by the skin of everyone's teeth.

Week five, Phase 5 began uneventfully, with the Oppressors herding the second batch of middle to upper-class people to take to the facility for testing. At this point, hundreds of children who struggled to remain with their mothers and fathers were murdered mercilessly by the invaders, and infants were no longer allowed to remain with mothers. The outcome of these babies remained unknown.

Many parents were also being killed for trying to protect their children. The number of those dying at the hands of the Oppressors was growing day by day. The number being actually taken to test was becoming less and less in contrast. What was going to happen when they came to those in authority and government workers, the last to be herded?

Josh and Kamryn had no time to consider these facts. She set about working hard on discovering the nature of their video system and learning how to access and control it. She was able to hack into their actual signal, and she disguised her presence effectively. Josh worked alongside her to rid his programs of any and all bugs.

They did a couple more tests on his program, and the final was successful. Not only were they going to be able to send a false signal to the ship above, but they were also going to be able to get it to every ship spanning the planet. Now, the only thing left to do was pinpoint their video system, and this was proving a bit more difficult than Kamryn wanted to admit.

Initially, all she was able to track down were records. Most of them unreadable without interpretation and that took time. They simply couldn't risk passing over visual feeds just because they didn't want to interpret the code patiently. This had to be done. It was frustrating and time-consuming, to say the least.

Next, she discovered countless voice records, once again all in the language of the Oppressors. These were bone-chilling. This was not the first planet they had carried out their selfish, morbid plans against. This had been going on for millennia, and from what they were able to understand, it would go on forever if someone didn't stop them.

She continued her search through their databases,

discovering that there was one main Mother Ship, and this ship was not in the Earth's atmosphere. It was in space, and it was the source of their signal. While this was invaluable information which would help her block their signal and substitute their own, it didn't help her at all when it came to tracking down the video.

Week six of the invasion focused once more on the middle class, and Superior announced to President Mason that week seven would see the beginning of herding the affluent and upper crust of the world, short the leaders. They anticipated this phase to last a mere two weeks, and they would clean up the escaped scraps of the lower and middle class during this time. They were devious and very, very patient.

Kamryn pressed on.

During day three of week six, Kamryn was the only one on the computer. Josh was at the cafeteria, and he would go to the gym and shower while she worked. She was learning how he felt when he was so pressured and working alone. She was mentally, physically, and emotionally exhausted. There was one thing she was pleased about. In only a couple of short weeks, she had learned enough about the Oppressors' language and programming systems to only need to call on interpretative services every now and then. As a matter of fact, she hadn't needed one at all in the last two days.

So, she continued to plug away, preparing passable satellite footage for each and every city around the globe which was overshadowed by the enemy's ships. She used footage only from specific periods of the day so the shadow of their ships could be simulated. By day five of week six, Kamryn had a fully prepared stock of mock video footage to feed into their system, once she was able to track it down specifically, that is.

With week six drawing to a close and the affluent preparing to be herded, Josh and Kamryn worked harder than ever. He mostly acted as her gofer. Whatever she needed he fetched, just as she had done when he was busy writing code. The arrangement worked well, and the stress Kamryn experienced only a week or two ago seemed to have dissipated into the abyss of her busyness.

"How is it going with tracking down their video?" Josh asked her in a low voice. He had learned not to loudly distract her; it would mean complete loss of her train of thought.

She sat back and let out a breath, stretching as she did. "There are only a few more signals to break down, and video has to be one of them. To be honest, I don't think the one I'm working on now is it, but with each failure, we are that much closer to success. Once I find it we can get things rolling. We have only a couple of weeks to act before it is our turn to go for testing." She turned her chair around to face him, palms flat on her thighs. "I'm confident. I just don't like pushing the envelope so much, you know?"

Josh nodded. "I have faith in you though, Kam."

"I know you do. It's very motivating, having someone believe in you. Not that I never had it before, but never in such a positive light. It's energizing." She smiled at him.

"I think we should take a half-hour to go get a bite to eat," Josh told her. "What do you say?"

"As long as it's only about a half-hour. I'm so close now that slowing down is not an option, and our time frame is pushing me pretty hard as well." She stood and willingly followed him out of the office.

They reached the cafeteria and got in line behind three other employees, each looking completely exhausted and haggard. They shuffled forward pushing their trays like zombies focused only on potential brains.

"I wonder if we look that rough…" Kamryn told Josh. "Would we even recognize it if we did? I haven't seen my own reflection in two days, which reminds me: I need a shower desperately."

"Take one when we are finished eating if you like," he replied.

Kam shook her head. "Not an option. Not today, anyway. I want to at least finish breaking down the feed I'm reading right now and get a leg up on the next before the day is out."

Josh chose a cheeseburger and soggy fries. He was sick to death of salad, and the last two he had were wilted and browning. He had noticed that what once had been wonderful food options here had slowly but surely become very poor. Regardless, he was in the mood for something with flavor rather than loads of nutrients.

Kamryn shared the same line of thought. She chose two small cardboard containers of chicken fingers and two containers of French fries. Aside from the potatoes, neither had any vegetables on their plates. Josh was surprised at her options. For a girl with a past, he had always admired her food choices. Now he admired her even more for going off the deep end with fat and calories. She certainly needed it.

They sat with their food after gathering condiments, and they began to inhale the sustenance, neither speaking. The only sounds coming from their table were their breathing and chewing. It was a peaceful, comfortable feeling for both of them.

They left the eatery feeling fat, sassy and rejuvenated. "I'm going to the gym and showers. You hitting the books again?" Josh asked as he walked her to the elevators.

"Yep. You know it. Can't back down now," she replied. At the elevator, she smiled at him, and he planted a kiss firmly on her lips.

"I'll see you soon, okay? Good luck, Kam."

Her grin broadened. "I'd tell you to break a leg, except you're going to the gym. Have a good workout and shower."

They parted ways, Kam getting on the elevator and Josh heading down the hall in the direction opposite the cafeteria. She watched him walk away until the doors closed.

She thought about Josh's family. Four days ago, he had attempted to call them, with no response. He had also tried some other family members to get information but to no avail. They both knew what that meant, but to come unglued over it was pointless. He shed minimal tears, but the pain still filled his eyes. In typical male fashion, he pressed on. She had held him and found as she comforted him that she was thinking of her own family, the family of long ago. She felt no pain or grief at the thought of anyone from her past being herded, and this made her feel a bit guilty, if not selfish.

Back in the office, she hit her tasks hard, and within an hour she had come to the solid conclusion that the latest signal she was breaking down had nothing to do with the video feed she was attempting to pinpoint. There were three remaining that she could detect, and she picked one at random to attack. After calling reception for a stiff pot of coffee, she began the deciphering process.

Josh returned shortly after she began, his dark curly hair wet and unruly. He looked refreshed, to say the least. Both of them had begun keeping their clothes in lockers downstairs, so they didn't have to haul things back and forth just to shower. Besides, laundry facilities were located on the same floor as the gym, and it made everything easier on them both.

She barely turned her attention from her computer when he returned, and he did his best not to distract her from her work. Rather, he grabbed his smartphone and began reading one of the many books he had downloaded onto it but hadn't read before. He wondered why he hadn't taken the time to read more before this all happened. So much in life, they had all taken for granted! The thought and the feelings it produced were indeed bittersweet.

His reading genres of choice were typically horror or science fiction, but those seemed like such tasteless options now. There was one book by an author who was known for self-help and improvement. His uncle had recommended it, and he had downloaded it to appease the man, never really intending to read it. Now it seemed pointless, but he felt compelled. Who knew? Maybe he would learn something and actually live long enough to apply it to his life.

He read for two hours straight, completely engrossed in the material, and finally, he pulled his eyes from the screen of his phone. He had nearly read himself into a trance! He needed to get the blood flowing again. He stood to stretch, and that was when he took notice of Kamryn. She was fast asleep, sitting in her desk chair, head and shoulders slumped over her keyboard. He smiled and watched her sleep for a moment. She was exhausted, but he had gotten to know her well enough to be aware that if he woke her to lie down, she would refuse. Instead, he gently picked her up from the chair, cradling her in his arms, and he laid her on the couch. He covered her with a blanket. She didn't stir.

Josh lay down on the floor next to her after lowering the office lights. She would be mad at him for not waking her, but the fact was that they were both worthless if not properly rested. He smiled to himself. She was adorable. She was beautiful, and if even for a very, very short time, she was his. He continued to smile as he set the alarm on his cell phone.

Within minutes he, too, was sleeping soundly.

∞

Day one of week seven saw the beginning of the herding for the affluent, and the continued searching on the part of the Oppressors for those who had managed to slip between their fingers. The number of people who had managed to go into hiding was amazing. Each day the enemy found scores of them all over the world, and it was anticipated that this would continue.

President Mason had met with Superior and his men yet again, this time to discuss their progress.

"As you know, we are nearing the completion of our process. Your people have been very cooperative, at least, considering it is not the nature of the life force to surrender freedom," Superior began. "This is the seventh week of the herding process, and we anticipate it will take two to three weeks to complete. At the end of that time, all levels of your governing authorities will be expected to surrender to the testing facilities."

Mason nodded, his stomach roiling violently with fear and apprehension. What really took place in those facilities? He thought he really didn't want to know, nor did he want to find out.

The truth of the matter was that the Oppressors had been honest. Testing was being conducted, and the strong would indeed be transported to a different planet to sustain the life of the human race. A number of flying crafts had been brought to the planet's surface, from where he was not sure. Their purpose was to transport those permitted to live, and some had already been taken there.

Mason asked, "Regarding the crafts, I was wondering if your men are flying us? If not, how will we navigate and operate them to get safely to our destination?"

"Very good inquiry and the fact that you ask makes me believe you are accepting the need to cooperate. I shall answer. They are programmed for self-flight, and your course is already known by the craft," Superior replied.

He continued. "Since we are nearing the end of our time together, it is essential that your remaining people put up as little resistance as possible. They will find the entire process much easier if they cooperate, as you have found. You all have an opportunity to continue life, just not on the planet of your birth."

Mason was done talking to him, but there was no point in acting like an ass. He continued to stand, listen, and nod compliantly, even offering a nod or tight-lipped smile now and then. Superior's reptilian eyes bore into him constantly, making him uncomfortable, but he refused to give away his discomfort.

"So, week seven begins and gathering the escapees continues. As I said, two to three weeks, President Mason, and you and the rest of the remaining people will begin their testing. This predicament is nearly over for all of us." He paused. "Emotion is not something we feel strongly, but we do experience it. Know that this has never been pleasant for us, at any time, under any circumstances."

Mason nodded once again. He highly doubted that it bothered the leader much, but if he felt he needed to reassure the Head of State, then Mason would kiss his ass and let him. He knew they had a plan, no matter how vague, in the works. He only hoped it came together completely soon.

Very soon.

The meeting had ended with Superior joining his lackeys, and Mason rejoining his. They discussed the words spoken and considered their own positions. They had a very short time to pull their plan completely together. If they did not, some would have to hide from the Oppressors in order to execute the plan and try to save humanity.

President Mason knew that his people at the Pentagon, including those two computer kids, were working non-stop. He received regular updates as to their progress, and he was fully aware that it was a process. Patience was their greatest strength at this time; it was certainly not the enemy. They all knew who the enemy truly was.

He looked up at his men. "Miles, contact Matthew Johnson at the Pentagon and get the latest word. The fact is, all we can do is bide our time." James nodded and stood, dialing his cell as he walked away from the men so he could have his conversation.

Mason began to wrap things up. "If ever we needed God, gentlemen, now is the time."

CHAPTER 16

Week Seven, Day Two

Kamryn was on a roll, and she knew it. She was plugging away at deciphering the second-to-last signal, and while it had been looking pretty grim, she was sure this was the video feed. As the old adage goes, what you are looking for is usually in the last place you look. Fortunately, it was second to last.

The bottom line was, she needed to be sure. She wanted a completely deciphered video signal feed. In her estimate, she was only hours away from having just that. She was wound up.

Once she completed this task, Josh would accompany her upstairs to Wells' office and let them know before they went forward with anything. They had a fake working signal to hack into the alien system with to distract it. She had put together a fake video feed made up of satellite images of each city. Now all she needed to do was be sure they would work by actually studying what the Oppressors' videos looked like. She knew she had jumped the gun a bit by developing the false footage without knowing what she was simulating, but the fact was she had to do something while Josh made sure he got rid of the bugs in his code writing. If she needed to tweak the footage, she would. No problem.

∞

Kamryn pounded away at the keyboard before her, and with each passing stroke, she grew closer and closer to the completion of her goal. She was sure she would have this deciphered and viewable by evening. It was now one o'clock in the afternoon.

Josh had gone down to eat. She hadn't been too eager to eat and opted to stay on task. She was glad because things were looking brighter and brighter with each passing second. Josh would bring her food, anyway. True to form, Josh opened the office door only moments later carrying a Styrofoam container of greasy pizza and a tall cup of ice cold soda.

He sat at his desk and began to spread out her meal for her. She barely glanced away from the screen to watch, but she knew he would make her take a short break if only long enough to eat what he had brought. She focused on finishing this leg of deciphering so she could fill her belly and get back to work.

In only minutes, she forced herself from the computer and turned to him smiling. She had not yet told him that she thought this was the video feed. She hadn't felt sure enough. The fact was, she wasn't finished, but she was sure. They needed the entire thing if they wanted to fake a replacement feed properly, of course, but she knew it was safe to tell him.

"Thank you for the pizza and pop, Josh. What did

you eat?" She found she was suddenly ravenous, even for the greasy-sponge pizza on the desk. She reached for a slice eagerly and took a large bite before looking to him for his response.

He observed pizza sauce on her chin and smiled. "The same, but I had three pieces. You have sauce on your chin." He chuckled.

"I know, I can feel it. I'm not even going to wipe it off until I'm done; I'll just do it again. I'm starved!" She took another huge bite.

He nodded. "You certainly are chipper, aren't you? It's good to see you smiling. You've been so focused on work, well, both of us have, that it seems we never laugh."

"I feel like I have something to laugh about."

His eyes widened slightly. "Really? What's that?"

"This is the Oppressor's video feed, Josh," she replied with a sauce-covered smile.

"You've got it?" He held his breath.

She nodded. "Yep."

"What's next?" He wanted to know everything. The look in his eyes gave his excitement away.

She chewed the pizza in her mouth, and reaching for a napkin, wiped her face before continuing. "I need to completely decipher it, so we have access to all footage they possess. Your deciphering code is working perfectly by the way. Once you finish the program, I will hack in, I need to compare the videos to what I have created, then make any necessary changes to ours that are needed to make it appear as much like theirs as possible. Once those two jobs are done, we head upstairs with our work. Voila!"

She half expected him to jump up and down, but instead, he let out a gust of air and sat back heavily in his chair. "I knew you could do it. I knew it, Kam. I just knew it."

"I'm guessing I'll be done by this evening at the very latest. I'm three-quarters of the way done now. I'm excited to see what they have on us. I'm even more excited to perfect the fakes and snowball these jerks." She tore back into her pizza hungrily.

His grin spread from ear to ear. "You eat. Enjoy. You certainly deserve it. Get us out of this, and I'll celebrate with you for the rest of my life!"

The smile ran away from her face. Did he just say what she thought he said? Did he just sort of… propose? Not one to make assumptions or jump the gun, she smiled again and continued chewing the bite that sat in her mouth.

"Okay, sounds like fun!"

She finished the food, guzzled half her soda, and excused herself to go to the bathroom.

∞

When she returned, Josh was studying the code on his computer. "I think the code is bug-free my love, the program is ready."

"Fantastic I can't wait to hack in, back to work for me," she said. He nodded and smiled in response before turning back to his screen. He was trying to be still so she could concentrate. For the next five hours, Kamryn plugged away at the deciphering process. This was definitely video, at least two months worth, if not more. They had only been herding for just under two months, so she assumed anything over that would consist of any monitoring of the human race they had been doing.

At five-seventeen, she finished. Josh was asleep on the couch, and she would not yet wake him. She wanted a sneak-peek before anyone else; after all, she deserved it. She hacked in, disguising herself carefully with Josh's program. It worked perfectly, she stole the entirety of the files, taking the next hour to download them, and that was using high-speed. Thank the Lord above they had not attacked back in the days when they were using dial-up here on Earth. What a disaster that would have been!

Just under an hour later, Kamryn began viewing what turned out to be surprisingly poor surveillance videos of planet Earth. They were grainy, and they were not in color. It would be almost too easy to fake what she had made to meet their needs; all too easy.

The most current ones, the ones from the present day, were no different. She could see that surveillance had not even begun until the ships arrived, so using satellite images from the darker evening hours had been the right choice. She could even identify most of the locations by site. This was looking better all the time.

She made herself pull away from the computer and turned her chair to look at the sleeping Josh. She smiled as she watched him breathe, his chest moving up and down. Suddenly she was filled with desire. What the heck? They could spare a little bit of time for the best thing in life.

She rose and walked to the door, locking it quietly as to not rouse him. She then removed her clothes and soft-stepped her way to him. She straddled his motionless form eagerly, and gently lowered her body down, sitting directly on him.

He stirred immediately, his eyes opening and struggling to focus. It didn't take him long. She began to unbutton his shirt, not taking her eyes from his. She could feel him growing progressively rock-hard beneath her. Wow, was she turned on! She leaned down and kissed him passionately, and he returned the favor, his hands tangling in her hair, his hips arching with excitement. She ground herself harder against him.

He then began to struggle to get his jeans off. Those things had to go now! She got off of him and knelt next to the couch so she could kiss him as he got naked. She then licked one of his nipples, even nipping at it a bit. He groaned and tried to sit up, but she acted fast, pushing him back down and straddling him once again. She would be in charge.

She directed him inside of her, and with a downward thrust of her hips—took him fiercely. He complied a pleased sigh, escaping him. She rode him hard, burying her face in his shoulder, then turning to seek out his eyes and mouth. He had a far-away look in his eyes. He was going to cum soon, and so was she.

Their movements grew increasingly more heated with each stroke. His hands ran feverishly up and down her back before grabbing tight to her butt cheeks and forcing her hips down hard on him. The action sent her over the edge, and she came with such force her toes curled. She sat up, grinding herself against him until she rode the wave of her own orgasm to full completion. She collapsed on top of him, her face once again buried in his shoulder.

"Wow, lady!" Josh finally spoke. "I take it you are done with the video!"

This made her laugh hard. "You bet your ass, mister, and it's all good."

"I want to see. Let's go."

They rose, cleaned up, and dressed. Once at the computer, she pulled up her downloaded files. They watched intently, discussing each and every video and individual shot. Josh was amazed at the shabbiness of the videos as well.

"I can't believe these guys have such a crappy camera system. That is what it is. Their computers are amazing. They must not watch TV or movies on their planet." He shook his head with disgust.

She was smiling and nodding. "That's my deduction, as well."

They watched until they didn't need to anymore. Kamryn spoke up, saying, "Give me an hour to apply some filtering to our fake files to make them appear lower-quality. Easy-breezy. Then we will call Wells."

R.W.K. Clark

CHAPTER 17

Peter Wells sat at his desk, staring at a painting on the far wall. The painting was the last thing on his mind. He was thinking about the entirety of his life.

How could a man with his education and military background feel so weak? He not only felt weak, he knew he was on the verge of pulling his own plug. Time was getting away from them all, and he wanted nothing to do with spending the rest of his life without his wife.

Week 7 was well under way, and he had not been able to get ahold of her at all.

The thought of what she may be going through made him ill. His stomach burned from the stress his imagination was giving him. He would rather die himself than arrive on some far-away planet only to discover she had not passed the testing. Did he really want her to face the future alone if she had passed? He was so confused, so torn.

He had allowed fleeting thoughts of suicide to pass through his mind before. He always quashed them; he believed that everyone experienced these thoughts, and carrying it out had simply never been an option.

Now it was more of an option than living. Almost.

His intercom buzzed, rudely jerking him out of his daze.

"Mr. Wells?" Sharon's voice echoed to him through the mechanism.

He sat forward. "Yes, Sharon."

"Mr. Nichols and Ms. Reynolds are here to see you."

"Show them in, please." He straightened his shirt, feeling for a tie that wasn't there. He then ran his fingers through his hair before weaving his fingers together in front of him. Couldn't look weak to the masses.

Josh and Kamryn entered his office, both smiling.

"Hello, Mr. Wells," Kamryn said. "How are you?"

Peter cleared his throat. "As good as can be expected. What's happening with the project?"

"That's why we're here." They both sat in the same chairs as always. "I have good news."

His face relaxed, and his eyes widened. "Let's hear it."

Josh sat back in his chair, allowing for Kamryn alone to have the floor. "I have isolated and deciphered their video feed, sir."

At first, it appeared that Wells was at a loss for words. After a moment of processing what she said, he finally spoke. "Tell me."

Kamryn proceeded to lay it all on the line. Not only had she isolated the video feed, but she and Josh had also viewed much of it as well. She explained the poor quality of the video and told him that she suspected their cameras were poor. She then told him she had doctored the fake video feed she had prepared to appear nearly identical in quality.

"It's all ready. All you need to do is move forward."

Wells didn't miss a beat. He grabbed the handset to his phone and punched in the necessary numbers. "Johnson, we're ready."

He hung up as quickly as he dialed. "Can you show me? Can you access it from my terminal?"

"I didn't save it to the cloud," she explained. "I wanted to keep things as safe as possible. We will need to either go to my terminal, or it will need to be installed up here."

Once again, he picked up his phone and dialed. "Hi, Ted. I need you and a couple of boys to go to Josh Nichols' office. Get Ms. Reynolds' computer terminal," he paused and looked at Kamryn. "Which desk is yours?"

"The one with all the paperwork on it right now," she replied.

He continued talking to Ted, the maintenance man. "It's the desk with all the paperwork. Bring her system up to my office stat and get the thing up and running." He hung up. "Johnson is contacting President Mason and the others. I'm guessing they will all be here shortly."

As if on cue, there was a sharp rap on his office door, and Johnson immediately entered. "I have them on their way." He looked at Josh. "Fill me in."

Kamryn spoke instead, explaining everything just as she had to Wells.

Matthew Johnson responded, "I want you to know

that the President told me via telephone that the leader contacted him one hour ago. They will begin herding government workers and authorities tomorrow."

The room went silent. Suddenly, Josh burst out, "That's at least one week early!"

"Yes, that's correct, but these characters haven't had a perfect track record when it comes to honesty, now have they?" Johnson continued, "We will gather forces and implement the plan while underground. We will take care of the technical side of things from here due to the high level of security. Forces will be kept in an undisclosed place until we have the video, the false signal, and all other aspects in place. Then we will attack. You two will stay here. It is vital that we resist if we want this to work."

The room fell silent. After only a few minutes, the office door opened, and President Mason and his three men entered the room, all three looking drastically as though they had seen better days.

"Give it to us," was the first thing out of his mouth.

Kamryn began filling them in, and by the time she was nearly finished, Ted and one of his guys were announced by Sharon through the intercom. In another twenty minutes, Kam was logging on and getting things up and running.

Together the group viewed the Oppressors' video feed in small, sporadic chunks. Then Kamryn proceeded to show them what she had prepared, showing them a small portion for each oppressed city. When she was done with that, she proceeded to show them the bare bones of uploading the false signal that would interfere with all their ships' programming and other capabilities.

"This will open the door for our attack," she concluded.

Mason spoke first. "We are sure this is going to work?"

"Nothing in this life is sure, President," Kamryn said. "But I'm betting my life on it."

The men all nodded together, as if on cue.

She continued, "I've only shown you the uploading process in case something happens to me. I already have all the necessary doors open. If for some reason I am captured in tomorrow's herding, you will still be able to execute the plan."

"Smart. Very smart," said Mason. They all returned to the circular formation which had become the norm for these meetings. "What's next, as far as you are concerned, Ms. Reynolds?"

Kamryn took only a minute to think before responding. "I will assume that herding us will begin at eight in the morning, just like all the other phases. It will be imperative that we all remain under lock and key, as well as your forces. I would take care of that immediately."

Carson Wood, the Secretary of Defense, spoke up. "The troops are all aware of the plan we have put together. The key now is to get them underground as soon as possible."

Josh said, "Think about it, gentlemen. The Oppressors are surely aware that the troops are our fighters. The President is surrounded by them by the hundreds when they meet; you have told us this yourself. I would be willing to bet they will want to herd the fighting men first and foremost."

This was obviously something the men in charge had not considered, but almost immediately Henry Whitaker nodded. "And I would be willing to bet you are absolutely right."

Once again silence fell on the room. When words were finally spoken, they came from President Mason. "When I spoke to Superior earlier, he said they still had to clean up a bit from the current phase. It is nine-thirty at night here, and I spoke to him at seven. I don't think it will be first thing in the morning, so we are going to violently press forward with our plan." He turned to Josh. "I want you two to get some sleep tonight. We will need you on your toes. Make sure you are up and at 'em by five in the morning."

Josh and Kamryn both nodded vigorously. He answered, "Not a problem, sir."

Mason then focused his attention on the other men. "The fact of the matter which is most important to face is that we don't know which of us are going to be captured or make it. We must proceed as if each and every one of us will live to see another day. This mindset will be imperative to our success as a nation, as a planet. Agreed?" Nods all around. "Good. Then plant those thoughts. Josh, if you two have anything you want to do, get moving. Leave the computer up here. We need to have access. Kamryn, do you have a back-up of the files?"

She smiled shyly, almost as if she had been caught doing something wrong. "Absolutely."

"Good girl, keep them safe. We will see you two in this office at 0500 hours." Mason dropped his hands into his lap, gesturing that he was finished.

Josh and Kamryn both stood. "Thank you," Josh said. "See you then."

In the elevator both of them were silent. While it was sinking in that the Oppressors had once again lied, neither of them felt that hope was entirely lost, and these were the thoughts they both were pondering. The fact was, they had done it. Together they had managed to come up with a solid plan to overthrow the enemy. It was magic, and it served to alleviate both of their fears by leaps and bounds.

Josh spoke. "I say we spend the evening celebrating, what do you say?"

Kamryn smiled broadly. "I would vehemently agree with you."

"Good," he replied. "I have a bottle of wine in my desk Wells gave me when I was hired on. I have never been a wine drinker, but tonight I am. It is supposed to be the best money can buy; they give one to all new hires."

They got off the elevator and headed for the office. Kamryn said, "I never got one!"

"I think they were pretty distracted when they took you on, Kam." They both laughed. Wasn't that the truth.

Once in the office, Kamryn got a lusty look on her face. "Josh."

He looked at her and recognized her bedroom eyes immediately. It made him smile.

"I'm going to get a shower. I'd ask you to join me, but we might get an audience. How about you do the same, and then we can grab some food and lock ourselves in here until it's time to rise? What do you say?"

"I'll meet you at the cafeteria in twenty minutes," Josh responded.

"Perfect, Big Guy."

They both headed back to the elevator and traveled down to the gym where they parted ways to their respective showering areas. Kamryn grabbed two towels, one for her body and one for her hair. She then headed to her locker and gathered her showering supplies: shampoo, body wash, and body sponge.

Once she was under the stream of steaming water, she began to consider where they were now as opposed to when this all began. She was so relieved that things had fallen into place. It was not about the job, no! It was about the fact that the job she had done could probably be accomplished by only a few people in the world. Had she ever doubted her ability to do it? If she were honest with herself, she would have to say yes. Deep inside, where no one went but her, she had many moments of personal doubt. She had only pressed on out of the challenge. She had been determined to overcome her own self-doubt, and that was what had driven her to succeed.

What could she have done with her life if she had focused that type of thinking properly? Well, it was a question that would remain forever unanswered. The past was gone.

∞

Josh stood in the shower lathering up. The water felt so good that he found himself wishing he could stand there, warm and clean, forever.

Then he thought about what Kamryn had for him, and he changed his mind fast.

Kamryn. She had to be the single most amazing woman he had ever met. Sure, she had a past, but man, she could do anything! She was so smart, and from what he knew about her background, she shouldn't be very well-spoken, but she was. She spoke to the President of the United States with all the confidence of one who had been bred to do so. Oh, and she was beautiful!

He shook his head in an attempt to clear her from his mind. He poured a bit of shampoo in his hand and applied it to his head. She had mentioned showering with him. What a thought! Visions of her body entered his mind: her flat stomach, slender legs, and those amazing breasts!

"Wow, Josh, focus. That way you can get out of here and have her right in front of you," he muttered to himself. He couldn't keep his mind on showering to save his life.

Finally, he gave up altogether and shut the stream of

hot water off. He walked over to the bench that ran along the wall and grabbed his towel. He began drying his hair and then the rest of his body.

He thought about the lies the Oppressors had consistently told. He thought about the facilities. He thought about the crafts which would transport those who passed the tests to their new home. What if they were only smoke and mirrors used as a weapon to instill false hope and incite cooperation on the part of the human race?

There was really no point in asking himself these questions. Mason had been right. Now was the time to believe that the battle was theirs. This was the only way to move forward, fearless and fighting. He set his mind; Kamryn had done it. She had put together everything they needed to move forward and attack not only the Oppressors hovering over Washington but all the others around the globe as well.

Once he was dressed, he headed for the door to the gym. Kamryn Reynolds, he thought, here I come.

CHAPTER 18

Kamryn stood outside the cafeteria waiting for Josh to arrive. For a man he sure takes a long time in the shower, she thought. Just then the elevator door opened and she watched him emerge. He sure was sexy. She could hardly wait to get him locked back inside the office. As hungry as she was, the hunger for food was nothing compared to her hunger for him.

Josh finally reached her. "Well, hello beautiful." His smile was wide. Just the sight of his perfect teeth brought a grin to her face.

"Thank you, gorgeous." They clasped their hands together and walked into the cafeteria, getting in line behind a couple of others. The place was dead.

This time they chose celebratory food. Josh selected two steaks that looked a bit warmed over, but they would have to do. Then they opted for baked potatoes and mixed vegetables, and for the first time, they chose two pieces of chocolate cake. Even though the food in the cafeteria was no longer as tasty or high-quality as it once was, it looked wonderful to both of them.

Both of the lovers opted for cold milk to drink. They will have wine soon enough, and besides, they would need it with the cake. They took their seats at a small table in a corner which seated only two. It seemed like a real date to Kamryn. She realized as she opened her napkin that she had never been on a date.

"Josh," she began.

"What's up?" He was already cutting into his steak. She began to doctor up her baked potato with butter, salt, and sour cream.

She blushed a bit and put her eyes on her potato. "I've never been on a date before." When he didn't answer, she looked up at him. He was staring at her with soft eyes. She was embarrassed. "Have you?"

Her voice was soft and shy, and he took notice right away.

"You know, Kam, I took a girl to prom in high school. That's it. To be honest, I have always been a bit of a nerd. I guess I can attribute my lack of a love life to that fact," he replied. "I was never ashamed of it, and neither should you be."

She gave him a smile, and her eyes thanked him.

"Maybe we could consider this a date," she said.

Josh made eye contact with her and firmly stated, "It already was in my mind."

They both laughed and began eating. Even if this were their last free night on Earth alive, they wouldn't have wanted to spend it any other way.

By the time they had cleared their plates, Kamryn wasn't even sure she had room for the cake. "I insist," Josh said. "What kind of date refuses to eat dessert with her man?"

"Certainly not me," Kamryn replied. "Gimme that fork. I'll show you the right way to eat a piece of chocolate cake." She cut off a massive chunk of the gooey concoction and shoved it into her mouth, getting frosting in both corners. Josh laughed. She was adorable.

But the cake did look amazing, and before he started in, he picked up the small paper plate it was on and took a big whiff. Before he knew what was happening, Kamryn gave the bottom of the plate a gentle slap. His nose hit the frosting, and a large glob of it remained there when he pulled the plate away.

"You little sneak! Wait until we get back to the office!" They both began laughing. It couldn't have been more perfect if the Oppressors had never arrived.

In another ten minutes, they were done, and they sat rubbing their tummies with satisfaction. It was nearly ten-thirty.

"Kam, I'm going to get us a couple of paper cups for the wine from up front. Meet you by the elevator?" He stood in expectation.

She nodded and wiped her mouth with her napkin. "See you there," she replied.

Kamryn didn't even make it to the elevator before Josh was by her side. All the way back to the office, they played and laughed like kids. The reality of the Oppressors and the future of the planet were the furthest things from their minds.

Superior was seated in his chair in the ship hovering over Washington, DC. To his right was Secondary, and Subordinate was at attention on his left. Neither was sitting; they were not permitted to. When you were in the presence of one in command, there was to be no relaxing of any kind. It was not acceptable. This strict form of discipline was conducive to control, as many of Earth's people had learned the hard way in the facilities.

Millions had been taken for testing to this point, and only a small fraction had been chosen for transport. It did not burden Superior's conscious in the slightest. This was how it had been done for the entire history of his planet and its people.

An American who worked for this government had come to him with information in hopes of sparing his own life. He had made them aware that he knew of a plan for the humans to overthrow the Oppressors. He could not give him details, but it was indeed in place. While they were able to monitor the humans with cameras and access their computers, Superior was certain they were missing something. This Mason, their leader, was far too cooperative in these last days. An underhanded plot did not surprise him at all.

Superior had told his minions to take the spy to the nearest facility for safe-keeping. He assured the traitor he would not have to undergo testing, but when he spoke to his minions alone, he ordered that the vermin be rushed through. "And see to it he fails." Disloyalty was the greatest sign of weakness in any life form. The man had taken a written education test, informed he had failed and was immediately terminated.

Now Superior sat in his chair, elbows on the armrests, fingers in a steeple-shape supporting his chin. He had contacted Mason, and they had met, and it was at that point he informed them of his intent to herd the government personnel and all in authority the following day. They would not wait another week to complete the process. The whole of the Oppressors could not risk it. Who knew what these insects were capable of?

He turned to Secondary, and in their native tongue, he spoke. "Can you theorize what they may be scheming?" He refused to let even the most minute amount of concern be heard in his voice.

Secondary made eye contact with his leader. "I do not see how it could be anything more than elementary, a childish attempt to escape their fate. They are nowhere near as advanced as our peoples! What can they possibly do to stop the process?"

Now Subordinate spoke. "We have no idea what they are capable of, and we all know it! All we have done is observe them since we arrived, and not that closely. We chose this planet based on its resources and the fact that they are remarkably similar to ourselves. We are foolish to think mutiny is not a real possibility!" His voice was riddled with anxiety because he knew he was right.

Superior stood, and with one lightning-fast motion, he retrieved his weapon from the holster at his thigh and blasted a hole in Subordinate that nearly took out his torso entirely. The underling fell to the ground like a bag full of dirt.

Superior replaced his weapon and calmly took his seat without batting an eye. Secondary shifted his stance nervously.

"If I may speak, I believe that regardless of what they have conjured up, you have made the decision to act in sufficient time. Things will go smoothly, Leader, watch and see," he said.

Superior ran the palm of his hand over his forehead, past his receding hairline, and down the length of his long blonde hair.

"For your sake, Secondary, I hope you are correct. Otherwise, you will be next. Get out of my sight."

The minion left his presence immediately, leaving the leader of their people to contemplate. While he could not conceive any plan which would succeed against the process, his heart knew that Subordinate was the honest one. He hadn't died for his honesty; he died for the tone he had used in responding. That would not be tolerated, and neither would mutiny on the part of these filthy creatures. If they had to use great force, they would wipe out the entire planet in one shot. It was that simple, and it would not be the first time they have had to handle it that way, either. So what if they lost Earth's resources? Didn't these idiots know they were lucky to be chosen? There were literally thousands of similar planets in this one little universe. It would be as easy as choosing another and beginning the process again.

He didn't mind. It was honestly all sport, which entertained him thoroughly.

R.W.K. Clark

CHAPTER 19

At four-fifteen the next morning, Kamryn and Josh lay on the floor of their office, green Army-issue wool blankets covering their naked bodies. Empty paper cups, which had contained the wine they had drained, lay tipped over on the floor next to them. They were wide awake, the reality of the Oppressors and of the day heavy on their sobering minds.

"Well, today is the day, supposedly. I wonder when they will come," Josh began.

Kamryn let out a sigh. She could honestly say she really wasn't petrified with fear anymore. Rather, she found herself sick with sadness and anger. She knew that when they came, she and Josh would be separated. She was also bleakly aware that she would likely never see him again, and these were the thoughts that sparked her emotions. They had only just found each other, and the fact that they would soon be ripped apart seemed downright criminal. In fact, it was.

"I won't give up without a fight, no matter when they come. The time doesn't matter, Josh. They are coming." She stood, the blanket wrapped around her, and walked to her desk to call reception for coffee. Josh began to get dressed, and she followed suit.

Ten minutes later, fully clothed, they were pouring coffee into cups and guzzling it with passion. They needed to clear the haze the wine had left in their brains as quickly as possible, and coffee was the answer. At least two cups apiece, probably more, would be needed.

At four-fifty the two left their office for the meeting with Wells and the others. The plan was for Kamryn to first hack into the video system aboard the ships. She would then begin to stream the false video feeds which she had engineered into the system, making it appear that their cameras were still picking up footage consistently. This must be done individually to each and every ship surrounding the planet because they had their own separate footage. Once the feeds were in place, she would send a block between the primary ship, located deeper in space, and the other ships. This must be done at the precise moment she sends up a dummy signal to operate the computers. If there is any system failure on any of the ships, it would be detected immediately, giving away the entire scheme. Once this step was complete, troops would storm onto the scene, both on the ground and in the air. That step was in the hands of the men in charge. She found herself concerned with foreign cities. Were they cooperating fully with their armed forces? She had to assume that they were; without their cooperation, there was absolutely no point in proceeding. Surely, the President and his men knew that.

They got off the elevator to see Sharon, the

secretary, dozing a bit at her desk. She had dark circles around her eyes, and it was obvious she had lost a good bit of weight during this ordeal, just as Kamryn had. The Oppressors and the situation they brought with them had taken a major toll on the entire planet.

They approached the desk quietly, not wanting to startle the woman. Softly, Josh said, "Sharon, we are here for the meeting."

Her head jerked upward, and she immediately turned red with embarrassment. "I'm so sorry. I must have nodded off for a second. Of course. The others are already here. There is coffee waiting inside. Go ahead." She smiled a bit and turned to her computer screen quickly to diffuse her humiliation.

"Thank you," Josh replied. He turned to Kamryn and smiled as he took her hand, guiding her to the office. He knocked twice and waited to hear the okay before entering.

Wells was at his desk, with the other men seated in a semi-circle around him in their usual positions. Only Josh's and Kamryn's seats were empty, waiting cold for them to warm them up.

"Good morning, you two. Thank you for always being so prompt. It is appreciated now more than ever," began Wells. "As you can see, we are all up and ready to go at 'em. Coffee?" He gestured to the rolling stand near the door, equipped with everything needed for a steep, hot cup of java. They headed to it before even considering taking a seat.

After a few moments, they made themselves comfortable, and the President began the conversation. "Kamryn, we know you have a technological plan of action. Can you give us a quick rundown again? We all need to be on the same page at all times if this is to succeed."

Kamryn covered the plan briefly. Upload false video feed one ship at a time, beginning with the one hovering over Washington. Then block their Mother signal while simultaneously putting out their own false one. This was the sensitive step, and she made sure they understood that clearly. It would only be after these steps that forces could advance.

"I assume you have the cooperation of overseas and foreign governments? I mean, they will have their troops and planes prepared, correct?" While this was not her problem, she felt compelled to ask.

Mason replied, "Absolutely, and they all have them underground, keeping them safe and sound until you give the go ahead. Kamryn, we have troops to fight for us, but this is essentially in your hands. It is important that you are fully aware of that. Are you?"

She was still, considering what he said. She hadn't thought of that fact, but that didn't change the truth. This was literally all riding on her. Her stomach fluttered violently, and goosebumps broke out on her skin. "Yes, sir, I am."

Josh reached over and took her hand, squeezing it gently. He had gotten to know her well, and he recognized nervousness in her eyes. She looked over at him, and he smiled and nodded in return. Then he turned to the men. "I can reassure you, Kamryn is not only fully aware of the level of responsibility she currently has, but she is also completely ready, capable of getting the job done right."

"Good," replied Mason. "We are all counting on you. Now, how much time are these steps going to take to complete in their entirety?"

Kamryn was using her mental calculator, ticking off minutes in her mind. Finally, she responded with a simple, "Four to five hours, tops, and I'm overestimating for safety's sake."

"Wonderful. They will try to herd our armed forces first. I am almost sure. At least, they will if they are operating with any intelligent kind of strategy, anyway. Therefore, I am confident we will have time for you to complete your portion of our plan." Mason paused, then continued, "I should add that our armed forces have been instructed to emerge from their places of hiding at a specific time, even if they have not received the order. That way, if we are all captured, yet have managed to complete the technological phase, they can come out and do their stuff in sufficient time. If we have not, they will still be able to choose their own course of action conducive to personal survival. I have instructed them to emerge at 1200 hours. Do you think you will be done by then for sure?"

Kamryn nodded vigorously and glanced at Wells' office clock. "I anticipate I will be done by ten o'clock at the very latest, sir, but I will know for sure around eight. I will give you a heads-up then in case you want to tweak the time frame a bit for military personnel."

All the men nodded, pleased. "Perfect," stated Mason. "Kamryn, we all want you to know how appreciative we are for the service you are doing for your country and for the world. It is invaluable, and we recognize that. Should this end the way we all hope, you will be handsomely compensated."

"Sir, let's just all get out of this mess alive, okay?" She sounded confident, but she really wanted to cry. It was not the execution of her plan which made her doubt; it was wondering whether any of them would survive.

Mason nodded yet again. "Well, then, we will let you get to work. I assume you will need your sidekick, Mr. Nichols. The rest of us are going to head down and pow-wow in the cafeteria for a bite. Have you two eaten? If not, we will have something brought up for you."

"Thank you, sir. That would be good," said Josh, smiling. He turned to Kamryn. "Ready, tiger?"

She nodded and grabbed her manila folder from the table next to her. It contained every piece of paperwork she had collected during the job, but she was certain she could complete the task without it. She had a mind like a steel trap.

They all rose, and Kamryn walked over to the station at which her computer sat: she looked it all over, took a deep breath, and sat down. As she booted up the system, the men left the room; Josh sat back down in his chair near Wells' desk, and we're off, she thought to herself as she typed her password into the computer.

R.W.K. Clark

CHAPTER 20

Kamryn sat at her computer station vigorously working, concentrating hard on uploading the first video feed. She wanted to upload the first one to the ship in Washington. While this seemed like an insane move due to the great risk involved, she knew it was the only way she would be able to find out if it worked right or not. If nothing seemed to change regarding the Oppressors' behavior, she would know that it had been a successful hack. If their behavior did change, well…

She had not shared this intent with the men. She believed they would not comprehend her thinking. They would want her to send the first feed to a different ship, but that could result in a delay of discovery, and as she continued with the upload process, all of the Oppressors would know her intent and come unglued. In her mind, this was the only way.

It was nearing five-thirty, and the first video feed was ready to be sent to the ship above. She was terribly nervous and had to force herself to tap the enter key. Her hand hovered over it for several seconds, finally tapping down hard. The upload began.

Within thirty seconds, it was complete. She clicked

her mouse on another tab which allowed her to view the ship's video feed, which she had already pulled up first and foremost. Sure enough, her feed was running successfully.

"The first video is up and running, Josh. On to the next." She didn't even look away from her screen. She simply went to work on the next.

Josh came over and watched over her shoulder as she feverishly worked. She was amazing. "How will we know if they identify it or not?"

She stopped then, but only long enough to answer him. "Because I sent the first feed to the ship over Washington. If we get word of chaos on the part of the Oppressors, well, then they will be onto us." She turned back to the system.

At twenty minutes to six, the phone on Wells' desk chirped loudly, making Josh jump. Kamryn seemed to not even hear it. With trepidation, Josh picked up the receiver and spoke. "Peter Wells' office."

"Josh, this is Peter. The final phase of the herding has already begun, and as we suspected, they have begun with military personnel. They are herding administrative workers first." Josh could hear a tremor in his voice.

He replied, "It's going to be fine. Kamryn successfully uploaded the first feed to the ship over Washington. She is partially through with the next. Please keep us posted on any change in the Oppressors' behavior that would signify that they recognize the video as being different, please."

"Will do. We are currently on the top floor. Have her keep pounding away. If you need us, we are at extension 742." Then Peter Wells was gone.

Five minutes later, Kamryn stated, "Done with number two. It's good." She continued to work.

Josh began pacing at this point. His armpits were beginning to sweat, as was his forehead. They were playing a very dangerous game, but when the stakes were human lives, what choice did any of them have?

Not even fifteen minutes passed before Kamryn announced the completion of the third upload, and within the next ninety minutes, all of the video feeds were replaced in every ship around the globe. She stood and stretched. Her eyes were lit with an excited fire.

"I can't believe how smoothly this is going so far. It worked perfectly, just the way I would want it to. I need a five-minute break." She began to pace in an effort to get her blood flowing. "Next, I will send the signal block to the mother ship, and at the precise moment I do, I will send up my false signal." She stopped pacing. She was looking at the window as though she had never seen one before.

"Josh, I never realized we were on the main floor here in Wells' office." She walked to the window and peeked out around the shade at its edge.

He nodded. "Yeah, we've been in this building for so long you probably just lost your bearings. But we are on the main floor. Why?"

"How safe are we really if we are on the main floor?" She turned to him with a stricken look in her eyes. "I need to get back to work. We may have no time to lose."

She sat back at her desk, and Josh watched over her shoulder as she pulled up a split screen and began to work off both, back and forth, one after the other. He watched her for a moment, then began to pace himself. She was right. If the Oppressors were going to clear out administrative personnel, wouldn't they consider government employees working at the Pentagon to be in that category?

After forty-five minutes Kamryn stopped tapping and spoke. "Josh, it's time," she said.

He had been at the window peeking out as she had. The Oppressors were dragging people, kicking and screaming, from someplace. Some of them were in government-issue uniform. Many of them wore traditional professional dress.

This was not good.

He turned to her. "Good, because I think these bastards are coming our way, Kam."

Her eyes widened, and he walked over to her. "Are you ready? If so, do it, babe."

She turned back to the computer, and with a shaking hand, she took hold of her mouse. "I have to click on one screen with the mouse to issue one command, and then immediately after, I have to manually press enter for the other command. I'm going to count backward from three; they must be done at the exact same time. Any error will glitch their system and give us away." Her voice trembled with her hands. "Count with me, Josh."

They began, "Three…"

There was a crash from somewhere in the building.

"Two…"

"One."

Kamryn clicked the mouse and the enter button together. It was done. The program was running.

"We did it, Josh. I have control of their ships."

Josh ran over and locked the door to the office. He began stacking office furniture against it while Kam tapped away like crazy. Now she was working on shutting down their guns.

"Hurry, Kam. They're in the building, I know it!"

As he worked to barricade them in, the office phone chirped. He ran to it and picked it up. "Yeah?"

"Josh, they have gained entrance into the Pentagon. Where are you two at with the plan?" Wells voice was tinged with panic.

"It's done. We have control, she is working on shutting down their weapons and communications. Tell forces to advance sooner. They can't wait until noon! I'm barricading the door, but I can hear a commotion. What do you want us to do?" He was breathing hard and keeping a close watch on the door.

Wells replied, "Keep working. When you are finished find a place to hide. I will tell Carson Wood to contact all branches of the armed forces. We will advance within the hour."

Josh hung up the phone and resumed building the barricade. "They are going to advance within the hour."

"Good," Kamryn replied. She turned from her

computer. "I have crippled their ability to communicate remotely, and I have shut down each ship's main weapon. I cannot control their personal arms though, Josh. It appears that those are independent. We will have to make do."

She rose and began helping him. They took everything off of Wells' desk and began to move it to the door as well. It was very heavy, and they had to use their full weight to get it across the room. They piled his mini-refrigerator, filing cabinet, and the small tables on that. Finally, they pushed the last chairs and a bookcase in front of all that. It was all they could do.

The sounds coming from outside the office were distant, but they were definitely the sounds of the Oppressors herding fighting people. "Kamryn, we need to get into the closet."

Without delay, she spun around and headed for it, stopping only to shut off the power to the computer screen and grab her manila envelope filled with notes. She didn't want them to have any access to information regarding what she had done. With that in hand, she headed into the closet, Josh right behind her. He closed the door, and in the darkness, he pushed her toward the very back of the closet.

He lit the screen on his smartphone so they would have light to look around. At the rear of the closet, there were three boxes stacked up. He moved around her and pushed them a short distance closer to the front. He then grabbed her arm. "We will crouch here, behind the boxes."

They got down, making themselves as small as possible. He made sure his cell was face down on the floor in case it lit up for any reason. They didn't speak. They just listened to the crashes, bangs, and screams coming from the distance outside of Wells' office.

But they were getting closer all the time. It was impossible to tell how close they really were. The only thing that could be discerned was the fact that the Oppressors were nearing them in their cramped little hiding place.

The hiding place with no way out.

∞

General Richard Fabriz addressed the hundreds of troops in the underground bunker in which he, too, was housed.

"Men! We will advance! Technological steps of the strategy have been completed, and in fifteen minutes, we will take the Oppressors. We know no fear; we fight for our lives and for the lives of those we love. We will take no prisoners, and not one of us will surrender to their herding efforts. Understood?"

"Yes, sir!"

He continued, "Stand at attention until I give the order."

The same thing was taking place in underground bunkers strategically placed all over the world. They were some of the best-kept secrets in existence, and now each and every member of the military was eternally grateful for them.

Men and women were led to the transport vehicles which would take them to the facilities where they would test. At the same time, men and women were being led out the back door of each facility. Some were put on small ships which would take them to their new home. Others were led to a building located behind the main facility. There they would be eliminated. Some appeared calm. Women sobbed. Others fought.

There was not one child among the masses.

CHAPTER 21

Superior sat in his chair calmly. He was speaking to Secondary, and though his demeanor was calm, his voice was harsh.

"Something indeed is wrong! I have not heard from one man in our army. When I attempt to communicate with them, I receive no response!"

Secondary was afraid to even speak. His mind continued to flash back to Subordinate's body as it crumpled to the floor, chest, and stomach all but gone.

"Leader, have you had your system team look into it?"

Superior growled loudly, and it seemed to come from the very depths of his being, making Secondary shudder with dread. "Yes! They are attempting to pinpoint any issues now. I fear these beings have truly had something up their sleeves all along!" He rose from his seat and began to pace about his sanctum. Just then another of his minions entered his quarters.

"Leader, we were in the midst of checking on communications when we discovered that our visuals have been… tampered with." The man was almost cowering with fear.

Calmly, with a still voice, Superior asked, "Tampered with?"

"Ye-ye-yes, Leader. They show the same visual as normal, but we can see none of our army or follow any of the herding whatsoever. It appears it is not the true visual." The minion took a step back, anticipating the reaction to come.

Superior raised his fists into the air and shook them violently. He took two long strides, and reaching the trembling minion, took him by the throat and squeezed.

The petty servant began to struggle against the leader's attack, but he was no match for the one before him. Superior had been trained in battle his entire existence, he had the upper hand.

"Explain, fool!" The servant tried to speak, but nothing came out of his mouth except spit and gurgling noises.

Superior grew even more agitated, his anger reaching its peak. With his other hand, he grabbed the servant by the top of his bald, narrow head and snapped his neck with one motion. He then looked the dead man in the eyes, amused with the way death felt in his bare hands. He dropped the body to the floor and turned to Secondary.

"Had I not known you since the beginning of my existence, you would be next for me, and this one has whet my appetite for blood. We will go to the surface together… now!" Secondary bowed in respect, then followed Superior out the door of his quarters.

They reached the control room in ten Earth minutes

flat. "We will be going to the planet's surface," stated Superior to the man at the controls. "Now!"

The ship's captain looked at him, terrified to open his mouth. Finally, he worked up enough courage to state, "I no longer have the power to open or close the doors, Leader."

Secondary backed toward the entrance to the control room. He would certainly make a run for it. When he saw the rage rising in his leader's eyes, he knew what was coming, and he knew his turn was coming up.

He ducked out the door and ran for his life.

∞

Josh and Kamryn were holding their breath trying to hear what was going on. The sounds of chaos had grown very close now.

Tears fell silently down Kamryn's cheeks. Josh held her hand firmly in his as they listened. "It's going to be alright, Kam," He whispered. "They won't find us. If they do, we will fight. I would rather die than be without you."

She nodded in the darkness, unbeknownst to him. Suddenly, they heard a blood-curdling shriek.

"No, no, we have more time!" It was Sharon's voice, right outside of Wells' office. "You said we had more time! No!" Her screams continued, soon becoming muffled. They continued but began to fade in the distance.

There was a crash. It was the Oppressors. They were

trying to get into the door of Wells' office.

Josh's arms went instinctively around Kamryn, and he pulled her close. She could hear his heart pounding, and she was sure they could hear it, too. Could they hear hers as well?

Crash! Again they stormed into the door. They were struggling against the barricade, but Josh knew in his heart that it was only a matter of time. He began to plant kiss after kiss on Kamryn's forehead and in her hair.

"I love you, Kamryn. I love you. I always will."

"I love you too, Josh. Forever," she replied. She squeezed her eyes tightly closed as the din continued to come from the outer office.

There was a deafening crash. They were through the door. Furnishings were being thrown; they could hear the pieces crashing against the wall of the office. Kamryn put her hands firmly over her ears.

Suddenly the closet door flew open and a blinding light shone directly on the two trembling young adults in the corner.

"Grrr..." was all the Oppressor in the lead said before rushing forward and grabbing Josh, whose arms were around Kamryn. He jerked him violently, trying to separate the two, but Kamryn clung to him.

She was sobbing, but she managed to scream over and over, "No! No! No, please no!" Another of the men crowded his way in and, grabbing her, ripped her from Josh's arms.

Kamryn took one look into his eyes and fainted

dead away.

∞

Kamryn woke to a loud clanging noise. What could that be? There was nothing in the office that would make that noise.

She rolled over and opened her eyes. She was in a large room. Pallet beds consisting of no more than covers, void of pillows, lined the walls. She sat up. There was a door at the end of the rectangular room, and next to it were two filthy toilets with sinks installed into the tanks of them, the kind you might see in a jail cell.

She was in a facility.

"Josh! Josh! Are you here?" Tears began to stream from her eyes.

A soft voice replied from a dark corner, "There is no one called Josh here."

She turned her head in the direction the voice came from. "Who is that? Where are we?"

A figure emerged from the shadows in a corner and began to slowly approach her. It was a girl, no more than seventeen years old. She was filthy, her clothing torn, and her hair in complete disarray. She held out her hand to Kamryn in a gesture of kindness.

"I'm Maddie. Maddie Anderson. We're in a facility."

"No!" Kamryn was in complete denial as to the reality of her situation.

Maddie sat down on the pallet next to Kamryn's. "What's your name?"

"My name is Kamryn, and I don't belong here. I

have to get out of here!" She stood and ran for the door. She began to pound viciously on the door. It was large and made of metal. It was not going to give way.

"It's no use, Kamryn. They won't even come to the door. They ignore us unless we are testing."

Kamryn fell to the floor, exasperated and exhausted. "Where is Josh? Where could he be?"

Maddie answered her question the best she could with the knowledge she had. "They keep men in another area of the facility. We don't even see them while we are testing. We see them only in the halls when we go for the tests."

Suddenly, Kamryn felt the tiniest sliver of hope.

"You mean, I might see him?" She asked Maddie.

The girl nodded in the darkness. "They took my dad and me at the same time. I have seen him in passing nearly every day, but we are not allowed to speak."

Kamryn's wheels began to turn. She needed to buck up. She needed to stay strong for Josh.

"When will they come to get us for the tests?"

∞

Josh was pacing around the filthy cell block. They had thrown him in, struggling every step of the way. He had landed on the floor, hitting his head in the process. He had only gotten up and chased after them, running into the large metal door as they slammed it in his face and locked it.

He had been in the room for what felt like days, but he knew it had been only a few hours. There were five other men with him, and one of them suggested he try to get some sleep, but he refused. How could anyone sleep under these circumstances?

All he could think about was Kamryn and the way she had gone limp like a rag doll in the arms of the Oppressor. What if they had killed her, or worse yet, raped her and left her alive? Where was she? The man who had told him to sleep also stated that if she were herded with him, she would be here also. He would see her before it was over when they went for testing. He had to come up with a plan.

∞

Superior was alone in his quarters. He was intellectually aware of what had taken place, generally anyway. Everyone who was on the ship was trapped on the ship. They could not figure out how to reverse the problem, or even what the nature of the problem was. The troops on Earth were continuing to herd, as far as he knew, and they would likely continue to do so until everyone was herded or they collapsed from exhaustion.

It really didn't matter at this point. He was sure that, whatever they had done to take down the ship's system was not the only measure they had taken. These beings were more than he had bargained for. Who knows what else they had put together as part of their scheme?

He had his minions working non-stop to try and fix the issues they had encountered, but it simply wasn't working. They could detect nothing amiss. Everything seemed to be working fine, but nothing was working at all.

Superior laughed bitterly. The end result would be bad for the Oppressors. Very bad.

He would almost bet his life they had military personnel in hiding, and that they were advancing as he paced. They would eliminate his armies quickly and easily. His armies were on foot, with only a single weapon apiece in their possession. These cockroaches had large machines which they could climb inside of and drive upon the surface of the ground. They could drive right over the top of his men.

Superior was mad. He always had been, since his body was tiny. He knew it, and he took great pride in the fact, he was a genocidal madman.

∞

General Fabriz had executed the orders given to him by the President perfectly.

Troops, both infantry and airmen, had been released on the Oppressors at 1000 hours exactly.

The war had begun, and as far as he could tell, the humans were winning.

∞

Kamryn, Maddie, and six other women who were being housed in Kamryn's cell were led out for testing. Maybe she would see Josh! As they were led down the cold, bare halls, she kept her eyes peeled. After five minutes of walking, they reached a room. The door was opened, and they were ushered inside.

"Find a place to sit," said an Oppressor at the front

of the room rudely.

Kamryn sat at a schoolroom desk which had papers on top. A sharpened pencil sat atop the papers. She looked at the Oppressor, who was writing on a clipboard of some kind. She didn't even have to think; the pencil went into the waistband of her pants without a second thought.

"Why aren't you testing?" The question was directed at her. She looked around and saw the others had begun to write on their papers. They looked at her out of the corner of their eyes, scared of being reprimanded themselves.

"I don't have a pencil," she replied timidly.

This seemed to infuriate the Oppressor. "Learn to solve problems! Get one from an empty desk, fool!"

She jumped up and grabbed the pencil from the desk next to hers, then she sat and began to take the test that sat before her, a smile on her face.

∞

Josh sat at the grimy, old-fashioned desk pretending to do their bidding, but he was really drawing stick figures. Stick figures of humans murdering other stick figures which were obviously Oppressors. The thought satisfied him deeply.

He knew what he would do. He had a plan, and it would be simple to carry out. He needed to be in the front of the line when they led them back to their cell.

He would risk dying for Kamryn.

The world outside of the facilities had nearly fallen completely apart, but the Oppressors were like robots in carrying out Superior's commands, and why not? They were terrified of him.

They had gotten no word to discontinue the herding or the testing, so they trudged away, but the fact was that the armies of this world were attacking them full force. They would shoot their weapons and take out the Earth soldiers, all the while continuing to drag people to the transport vehicles. Shouldn't Superior have come to their aid by now?

Trudge was one of the Oppressor soldiers toiling away at carrying out his herding orders. He was a good military man, and loyal to the army and the Leader. He had a female Earth being slung over his shoulder. He had knocked her out cold with a single punch to the head, and on the way to the transport vehicle, he had managed to kill several Earth soldiers. He was very proud of himself and smug, but fighting was going on all around him; they were losing control, and it looked like all his work would be for naught.

He heard a terrible noise, metallic and ripping in nature. It came from overhead. He looked up just in time to see an Earth airship use its weapons on the Oppressor ship, tearing a massive hole in its hull. Flames and sparks shot out of the massive vessel, and a large chunk of its hull fell heavily to the ground. It was as big as a house, and it landed directly on Trudge and several other Oppressors and Earthlings alike, killing everyone it landed on. He didn't even have time to wonder what was happening.

The same thing was taking place all over the world.

∞

Kamryn and the other women were being escorted back to their cell to have 'sustenance,' as the Oppressors called it. She had taken the front of the line, and as they walked, she took note of the keys and the weapon at the Oppressor's side.

She closed the distance between herself and the inhuman being before her rapidly, not giving herself time to think or be afraid. As she picked up her pace, she took the sharpened pencil from the waistband of her dirty jeans, and as the gap between them closed, she lifted the makeshift weapon over her head. With all her might, she plunged it between his shoulder blades and slightly to the left of his spine. It entered his body like a hot knife in butter.

She pulled back and quickly repeated her violent act. The Oppressor fell to his knees, his head back, his mouth open in agony. When he fell forward to his face, she stabbed him again and again, until finally, she was sure he was dead.

She took the keys from his belt and, turning to the other women, said simply, "Follow me, quick!"

They ran as fast as they could, looking for any door that would lead them out of the horrid facility.

At the exact same time that Kamryn was pulling the pencil from her jeans, Josh himself was closing his own gap. He was tightening the space between the Oppressor leading the men to their cells, but he didn't have a pencil. In a flash, he reached forward and tore the weapon from the thigh of the alien being leading the line. Josh had no idea how to work the thing, so he simply aimed and pressed the only button he could see. It worked like a charm. The weapon emitted a line of light from a ball of fire at its muzzle, and it succeeded in ripping the being in two. The Oppressor fell directly to the floor, dead.

Josh looked at the weapon in his hand, observing the string of smoke which came from what he could only assume was a barrel. "Damn…" was the only thing he could think of to say. He turned to the others. "If you want out as bad as I do, I'd take your chance now, guys."

He turned and took off running to find Kamryn.

∞

The facility was a maze of insane twists and turns which seemed to lead only to the metal doors of the cells. Kamryn could find no clearly marked exit, and she was beginning to panic; so were the women behind her. Suddenly, she heard her name.

"Kamryn! Kamryn! Are you in there?" Her eyes lit up. "Josh?" She screamed it as loud as she could. "Josh!"

They both continued yelling each other's names, getting closer and closer, until Kam turned a corner and plowed directly into him. "Kamryn!" He took her in his arms and squeezed her tightly to him. He then released her, saying, "We have to get out of here now!" He took her hand and led her and the other women down a long hallway.

Suddenly, in a hallway to their right, an Oppressor appeared standing only about twenty yards away. "Stop! Where is your Director? You must return to your quarters, humans!" He began to make his way to them quickly.

"Run!" The group of women, led by Josh, continued their original course. They turned right, then left, then left again.

"Do you know where we are going, Josh?" Kamryn was beginning to get a bit desperate.

He nodded at her. "I do. I was awake when they brought me."

They turned another three times, and then right in front of them, like magic, was an open door. Right outside of it, there were a number of small ships. There were also some kicking, fighting humans struggling against the Oppressors who tried to maintain their arrest.

The group ran out the door and stopped dead in their tracks. Josh was staring, open-mouthed, at the sky above.

The Oppressors' ship was breaking apart, massive chunks of it falling from the sky and hitting the Earth in random places all around.

Surrounded by Oppressors closing in fast, "We have to take a ship, or we are all going to die." Josh began to run for the closest small craft. It was running and appeared to be lighting up. The entrance was open, but it was beginning to close. Kamryn took notice that all the small ships were full and preparing to take off. "Get in. Everyone, IN!"

They ran up the walkway and into the ship. The last two women, who had been lagging behind slightly, did not make it, however. When Kamryn got on board, she turned to take their hands and help them, but they were both crushed by a piece of the burning Oppressor ship.

The door of the transport craft seal shut with a loud 'SUCK.' It was airtight.

It lifted directly off the ground and began to vibrate wildly. Kamryn looked around. There were approximately twenty people aboard with her and Josh, and as the craft headed into space, she turned to him and asked, "Where are we going, Josh?"

A voice from the back of the craft answered her question.

"Our new home."

EPILOGUE

General Fabriz and President Mason observed the rubble and destruction all around them. Everything was flaming, smoke, and ashes. Every now and then a hand would wave from the piles of metal and debris, and another person would be saved.

Most of the Earth was in the same state. The death toll from the destruction was inconceivable. Humans had a lot of work ahead of them.

Years' and years' worth.

The earth was burning and smoking. The bodies of humans and Oppressors alike were littering the entire landscape.

∞

The mini-craft flew far above the earth, far out of its atmosphere. It continued to distance itself from the smoking planet and its mangled inhabitants. Josh wondered how it flew. There were no Oppressors aboard.

Everyone was asleep, including Kamryn. There had been blankets at each seat, and he had found more in a storage space on one wall. He covered Kamryn and the extra women with them and went to explore.

He found bathroom facilities, an abundance of non-perishable food and water, and a cockpit. That is what he had been looking for. He entered the area and observed the lights and gauges. He couldn't comprehend anything he was seeing. Nothing, that is, but one thing.

Digital red lights, in four sections of two each. The red flashing figures in each one changed with each flash. It was counting down. Counting down to their arrival at the planet they were heading to. Even though he couldn't decipher the numbers, he was fully aware that was exactly what it was doing.

How long would they fly?

He stood and stared at the vast expanse of space spread out before them. He knew Kamryn was approaching before she even wrapped her arms around him and hugged him tightly to her.

"How long until we get there?" she asked.

He looked again at the clock. Four sections of two.

"I would be willing to bet that it will be a while, Kam." He turned to her. "But we're together, and that's all that matters to me. We're alive, and we're together."

He kissed her lips and held her tightly to him. Together, they gazed in awe at the universe before them.

They would simply begin life again.

Overtaken

ENTREATY

This book was made possible by reviews from readers like you. Reviews fuel my creativity. If you enjoyed this novel, I implore you to please write a review and share your experience on the retailer's website. The livelihood for authors is entirely dependent on reviews, and I must say, it is the largest obstacle as a struggling author that I have encountered. Please tell a friend, tell a loved one about this read. With your help, I will be one step closer to overcoming this obstacle. In return, I thank you from the bottom of my heart, and sincerely appreciate your time and effort.

Humbled, with gratitude,

R.W.K. Clark

ABOUT THE AUTHOR

I am a father of two beautiful children, Jon and Kim. They are my motivating forces; they are the lighthouse in this vast ocean. In my life, they are the air that I breathe; they are the oasis in this desert of uncertainty. They are my greatest joy in life and my number one priority. I have a long list of hobbies, and I attribute that to my lust for life! I like to surround myself with positive people, who share the same interests. Family values, the arts, outdoors, nature, and travel are tops on my list. I embrace attending cultural and artistic events because I believe dramatic self-expression is the window to the soul. I wear my heart on my sleeve, and I still believe in chivalry, and I always treat people the way I want to be treated.

www.rwkclark.com